THE FABULOUS FOUR
FISH FINGERS

JASON BERESFORD

THE FABULOUS FOUR FISH FINGERS

JASON BERESFORD

Catnip

To Mum, Dad, Hayley and Laura.
Without them there wouldn't be a
funny bone in my body.

CATNIP BOOKS
Published by Catnip Publishing Ltd
Quality Court, off Chancery Lane
London
WC2A 1HR

This edition first published 2013

1 3 5 7 9 10 8 6 4 2

Text copyright © Jason Beresford, 2013
Cover design and illustrations © Vicky Barker

The moral right of the author has been asserted.

A CIP catalogue record for this book is available from the British Library.

ISBN 978-1-84647-1681

Printed and bound by CPI Group (UK) Ltd, Croydon, CR0 4YY

www.catnippublishing.co.uk

THE HOLE

Tumchester prison housed some of the meanest, ugliest criminals ever to crawl the earth. Crooks like Father XXXmas (the fake Santa with maggots in his beard), Knuckles McLucky (the three-armed bandit) and Theresa the Sneezer (who blew germs from her nose with the force of a hurricane).

But there was one crook so nasty his name was spoken only in whispers. He was locked behind a gigantic steel door and he scared the living daylights out of the guards as well as all the other prisoners.

He was known as The Panteater. He looked like an anteater, walked like an anteater and smelled like an anteater – but he was allergic to ants. So he ate pants. Cotton pants, nylon pants, pants with elastic, pants with frilly bits, stretchy pants, silky pants, stripy pants, spotty pants, Spider-Man pants. Even pants with holes in. Even pants that had been on for a few days and needed a good wash.

The Panteater hadn't tasted his favourite food

since they locked him in jail, but he wouldn't have to wait much longer . . .

Prison Officer Stan Button stared through the peephole in The Panteater's cell door and shook his head. Tumchester's most infamous baddie was crouched down inside a little tent, putting on a puppet show. He had one hand stuffed in a rubber crocodile and the other in a policeman. Suddenly, the policeman started bashing the crocodile on the head with a sausage.

'You're a very, very naughty boy,' he yelled.

The crocodile shouted, 'So are you!' and slapped the policeman in the face with a sardine. Then the crocodile said, 'It's time for a kip,' and both puppets hopped into bed and went to sleep.

The Panteater had told Stan he wanted to put on shows for kids when he got out of jail so he needed the tent and the puppets to practise. But this was the worst show Stan had ever seen (and that was saying something because he'd watched The Panteater do the same silly thing for weeks). The guard carried on his rounds.

An hour later, Stan came back and peered through The Panteater's peephole again. The puppets were *still* snoozing. *Something smells a bit fishy to me*, he thought, *and I don't mean that crocodile's breath*. Stan marched sternly into the cell, but before he could speak he noticed something peculiar on the wall behind the tent. A hole. A big hole. A Panteater-sized hole. 'Oh n-n-n-no!' stuttered the guard. 'He's out!'

Soon alarms were ringing, whistles were blowing and every guard in Tumchester prison was out searching for The Panteater. Except for Stan, who was left in the cell trying to figure out what had happened. He stared at the hole and the pile of bricks and scratched his head. How could something as big as a Panteater escape without showing up on the CCTV?

Poor Stan never thought to look *underneath* the tent. If he had, he might have noticed another Panteater-sized hole in the floorboards. And he might have seen Tumchester's hairiest, scariest crook hiding there, silently licking his lips.

The guard didn't know what hit him. The Panteater's tongue shot up his trouser leg like a boa constrictor and wrapped itself around his undies in a blink.

Stan screamed, 'WAAAAAAAAAAHH!' while the villain swallowed his pants in a single gulp. The guard lay quivering on the floor as The Panteater stole his uniform and rolled him up in the tent. Stan would feel much better in about ten minutes, but that was all the time The Panteater needed. He pulled his new hat down low over his face and walked out with Stan's keys jangling in his pocket.

OUR HEROES

The Tumchester clock struck four as Morris and Gary sprinted out through the gates of Fish Street School.

The boys had been best mates since they were born in the same hospital on the same day. Gary Gamble was older by thirty-three minutes and these days he was also taller by thirty-three centimetres (if you included his blonde hair that he spiked up with gel). Morris Twiddle's brown, curly hair didn't suit gel. It just made him look like he'd gone through a car wash on his scooter, so he never bothered with it.

Today they were off to battle the flesh-eating zombies who lived in the field by the school. These 'zombies' were also known as stinging nettles and in the summer the two friends spent hours whacking them with intergalactic death spears (also known as sticks). The enemy were down to one last patch by an old house on the far side of the field. The house was so creepy that Morris and Gary had kept well away until now. But in its long, dark shadows grew the tallest nettles the boys had ever seen.

'For that, Mr Zombie Trousers, you will pay with your life,' shouted Morris, slicing a nettle in two.

'And I don't know why *you're* smiling,' yelled Gary, chopping another. 'Try laughing your head off now you haven't got one!'

It was all going well until Morris cried, 'Aagghh! Captain, I've been hit! Think I'm going to lose a leg.'

'Never mind, it'll save you a fortune in socks,' chuckled Gary.

Morris sat down to rub a dock leaf on his knee. 'That's the last time I wear shorts to a zombie fight,' he moaned.

At that moment, Bel and Ruby strolled into the field pushing a pram. From a distance they looked like two girls out playing Mummies, but they hadn't brought any dolls or babies with them. Only a big, green, hungry parrot called Marvin who was shrieking 'MAAAARVIN'S STAAAARVIN!' even though he'd just had his tea. Not to mention his breakfast, his lunch and an afternoon snack of two coconuts, three cheese sandwiches, a plate of spaghetti, a packet of cornflakes (including the packet) and a watermelon so big it could have been used as a basketball by a team of brontosauruses.

Gary shouted, 'Cease fire!' as the girls ran over with Marvin's cage jiggling on top of the pram.

'How's the war going?' asked Ruby.

'Casualties on both sides,' said Morris, still nursing his knee.

'You two fancy saving the world again?' asked Gary.

'Ooh, thanks very much,' said Bel, seizing a stick.

'Thought you'd never ask!' said Ruby and the girls quickly joined the fight.

Bel Singh's parents came from India and her skin was smooth and dark, while Ruby Rudd's was paler than milk. Bel's hair was long and Ruby's was kept short under a funky hat; Bel's nails were painted and Ruby's were chewed. But differences like those don't matter to best friends and the girls had plenty of other things in common. Top of the list was a love of slaying zombies.

'Jeepers creepers,' said Ruby, who lived with her gran and sometimes spoke like she was eighty-seven. 'These zombies are tough as old turnips!'

'Good job the Fish Fingers are here to save the world,' said Bel. The four children had called themselves the Fish Fingers since they were small. It had been Ruby's idea because, she pointed out, they all lived on Fish Street. And they all had fingers.

'Hey, Marvin,' Ruby called out, bouncing around as if she was on a trampoline. 'If you're still staaarving, how about fried zombie for tea?'

Ruby turned to look at her parrot, but Marvin's

cage was empty and the door was hanging open.

'Oh no!' she cried. **'MARVIN!'**

The children dropped their sticks.

'Come on,' said Gary, picking up the cage. 'We'll find him.'

'The bumps in the field must have shaken the door open,' said Bel.

'What if he's flown back to Africa?' asked Ruby.

'He's not jet-propelled,' said Morris. 'He can't have got that far.'

Luckily, it didn't take long to track Marvin down. He was sitting on the roof of the sinister old house squawking, 'MAAAARVIN'S STAAAARVIN!'

'My giddy aunt,' Ruby gasped. 'I don't fancy going in there.'

The house was surrounded by a high fence topped with barbed wire and there were signs saying **DANGER** and **FOR DEMOLITION**. It was the last place in Tumchester the children wanted to explore, but they didn't have much choice if they were going to catch that parrot.

Gary found some broken planks and they sneaked through the gap. Marvin was hopping across the guttering on the roof and whistling merrily.

'Down you come, little chap,' said Bel, but Marvin pretended he was Santa Claus and leapt down the chimney instead.

12

'Disaster,' said Morris.

'We have to go inside,' said Gary.

The girls gulped, then Ruby nodded and so did Bel. (Bel would have followed Ruby anywhere. Unless she was going somewhere with rabbits. Even thinking about rabbits gave Bel goosebumps.) Morris had the jitters too, but he wasn't about to admit it.

'It's bound to be locked,' Morris said, hoping he was right, but Gary climbed the steps anyway. He gave the door a shove and to everybody's surprise, it swung open.

The four children walked slowly across the floorboards, treading through dust and bits of gravel that looked like little teeth.

'This place is crumbling to bits,' said Morris as Ruby bit her fingernails.

'Marvin, where are you?' she called nervously, but her voice just echoed off the damp walls.

As their eyes got used to the gloom, the children got braver and entered the living room. There were cobwebs everywhere, curtains with holes at the windows and a very old-fashioned record player in the corner. It was decorated with tiny carvings of bluebells and toadstools and there was a big brass horn sticking out of the top. There was also a shiny handle on the side and Marvin was using this for a perch.

'MAAAARVIN'S STAAAARVIN!' he squawked.

The four pals circled the record player and Ruby whispered, 'Come on, boy.'

The parrot gave a little chirrup, as if to say he didn't know what all the fuss was about, flapped his wings and hopped on to Ruby's shoulder.

'Welcome home,' sighed Ruby. 'But don't do that to me again.'

'Come on,' said Morris. 'Before we get caught.'

'Just a sec,' said Bel. 'Don't you think the record player's amazing?'

'Er, what's a record player?' asked Gary.

'This is,' said Ruby, blowing dust off the lid. 'My gran has got one. It plays music.'

'Very nice,' said Gary. 'Not as cool as an MP3 though. You'd look well stupid carrying that around the playground.'

'We really need to go,' said Morris, who was now getting the shivers on top of the jitters.

'Look, there's a record as well,' said Bel. 'Let's see if it plays.'

Morris let out a breath. 'If we have to,' he sighed.

Ruby wound the handle and put the record on the turntable. As it started to spin, she lowered a metal arm with a needle on the end down into the grooves of the record. Soon they could hear tiny sounds coming from the brass horn.

tiddly pom tiddly pom tiddly pom pom pom . . .

'Oooh, that's lovely,' said Bel. It made her think of fireflies and moonbeams.

'Smashing,' said Ruby, who thought she could smell strawberries and apricots.

tiddly pom tiddly pom tiddly pom pom pom . . .

'Sounds like a cat with its head stuck in a trumpet to me,' said Morris.

'Bit quiet, though, isn't it?' said Gary and he peered inside the horn. 'Hang on,' he said, sticking his fingers in and pulling out a ball of fluff.

TIDDLY POM TIDDLY POM TIDDLY POM POM POM...

It was much louder now.

TIDDLY POM TIDDLY POM TIDDLY POM POM POM...

Spirits lifted by the music, the children began to dance, but then—

TIDDLY POM POM sssss-K-K-K-K!

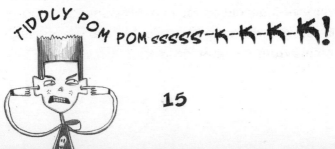

15

The sudden scraping noise startled them. It was the needle, jammed in the middle of the record.

'*Now* can we go?' said Morris. 'This place is way too creepy.'

The four friends raced outside and ducked under the fence. Ruby put Marvin back in his cage on the pram and they all went to sit under an oak tree in the middle of the field. It was only then that Gary remembered he'd stuffed the ball of fluff in his pocket. He pulled it out, gave it a shake and found it had ears and a nose.

'Wowzer!' he said. 'Check this out.'

'It's not a dead rabbit is it?' asked Bel.

'No,' said Gary, wiping the dirt from its little face. 'It's . . . a teddy bear.'

The bear had a miniature mobile phone in its paw and there was a sticker on the back that read:

IF FOUND PLEASE DIAL 27-33-36-61

'Sounds like bingo numbers,' said Ruby.

'I tell you what's strange,' said Bel. 'They're the same as our house numbers. It starts with Gary's, then mine, Ruby's, and Morris's.'

The children felt the hairs on the back of their necks stand up.

'It's turning out to be a very freaky Friday,' said Morris.

'I'm going to call it,' said Gary, pressing the tiny

16

numbers on the phone. 'There might be a reward.'

They all huddled in, but there wasn't even a crackle. Just a long silence. Morris was about to say, 'I knew it was a joke,' but it came out as 'I knew it was **AAAAARRGGHH!**' because there was a flash, a bang, and a cloud of white smoke.

A man the size of a penguin now stood before them. He was wearing a Viking helmet, flip flops and a purple tracksuit. He had a big nose and he was eating a packet of crisps.

A BAD HARE DAY

On the other side of Tumchester, Terry Simpson was in his sweet shop, polishing a jar of jelly snakes with the sleeve of his jumper, when the door opened. It made a dingle-dangle noise and Mr Simpson saw a tall figure come in. He guessed that whoever it was must be going to a costume party dressed as a pirate. Or a rabbit. Or both. (Terry thought this because there was a patch over the man's eye and he looked quite rabbity.)

The man-rabbit-pirate-thing said, 'Have you got any carrots?' which was not what Mr Simpson was expecting. After all, it was a sweet shop.

Before Mr Simpson could answer, the man-rabbit-pirate-thing leapt into the air and let out a hideous scream. Then it shoved the shopkeeper's knees up under his woolly jumper, pulled his arms out of the sleeves and tied the sleeves round his waist. The attack was over in less time than it takes a bald man to comb his hair. Mr Simpson opened his mouth to protest, but the man-rabbit-pirate-thing shoved a

giant gobstopper in it and started filling up plastic
bags with stolen sweets. Once the bags were full, he
headed for the door.

'Such excellent customer service and what cheap
prices!' laughed the crook. 'I'll be back again next
time you've got a sale on!'

Mr Simpson replied, 'Mmmnnwhumppphhh!' He was
left rolling around the floor trussed up like a turkey
– the latest victim of the evil supervillain known as
Jumper Jack Flash. And Mr Simpson wouldn't be the
last . . .

GOOD ELF

The children were standing with their mouths open and their eyes bobbing in their sockets like bouncy balls.

The little man with the crisps screamed, '**MR SNUGGLES!**' and rushed over to give the teddy bear a big kiss and a cuddle.

Because it seemed like someone should speak, Gary said, 'Er, we found him in an old record player.'

'And we rang the number on the phone,' added Ruby.

'Thanks very much,' said the man, still hugging the bear. 'I put him in a safe place fifty years ago and then forgot where my safe place was! I do it with my glasses all the time. I did it once with my Aunty Gladys. You didn't find her inside that record player as well, did you?'

The children looked at each other and blinked. It was all very confusing.

'Guess not then,' said the man. 'Sorry, I'm being rude. Let me introduce myself. I'm Cyril and you have just hit the jackpot because I am . . . Wait for it . . .' (Cyril twirled his arm like a propeller) '. . . Drumroll somebody . . .' (more twirling) '. . . An elf!'

'We don't believe in elves,' said Gary.

'I think you were hiding behind that tree with a firework,' said Bel.

'Wow. Tough crowd,' said Cyril.

'If you were an elf, you'd have a beard,' said Ruby, her eyes narrowing.

'I like a shave in the morning!' said Cyril. 'Doesn't make me less of an elf. And I might not have a beard, but I've got crisps!'

'Are they magic elf crisps sprinkled in starlight?' asked Ruby.

'No, salt and vinegar,' said Cyril, finishing the packet.

'I think you're a weirdo,' said Morris. 'We're not supposed to talk to weirdos.'

Cyril was getting into a huff.

'Kids today, you need proof before you believe in anything. Right. Stand back.' He held up his arms and huge bolts of green lightning shot from his fingertips. 'Get a load of this!' he shouted.

The lightning bolt hit a tree which exploded into flames. Out of the fire pounced a giant five-headed dog, as tall as an electricity pylon. It stood on its hind legs and bit the top off a lamp post before leaping towards the children, stretching out its claws and gnashing its teeth. Gary, Bel, Ruby and Morris screamed, but before the dog could swallow them up, Cyril clicked his fingers and it disappeared.

They all believed in elves a lot more now.

Cyril didn't tell them he'd actually meant to turn the tree into a bowl of goldfish, rather than a five-headed dog. No one needed to know.

'Have I told you about the wish yet?' he asked quickly.

'W-wish?' said Gary.

'Oh yes,' said Cyril. 'Under elf law I have to grant you a wish for finding Mr Snuggles.'

'D-do we get one each?' asked Bel.

'No, or we'd be here till Christmas,' said Cyril. He looked around. 'And it's summer, right?'

They nodded.

'So that's a loooooooooong time to wait. Better

22

to have a really big wish between you.' He winked. 'Now make it a brilliant one!'

The children knew they could wish for anything in the universe, but this made it *more* tricky. There was just too much choice. They had enough trouble making up their minds about what to have for tea or what to wear at the weekend, so they really couldn't think.

Then Morris said, 'How about the biggest, most fantastic doughnut ever created, with strawberries, pineapple, chocolate and mint-choc-chip ice-cream in the middle.'

'I can't stand mint-choc-chip,' said Gary.

'And I'm allergic to pineapple,' said Bel.

'I'd rather have something cheesy,' said Ruby. 'With chips and curry.'

'Right-o,' said Morris. 'Forget the doughnut. We can think of something else.' Except he couldn't now because his head was full of doughnuts.

Everybody said 'Um . . .' and 'Er . . .' for a very long time. Until Gary had the most incredible idea he'd ever had. An idea so incredible that it would change not only the lives of the Fish Fingers, but the future of Tumchester . . .

ANIMAL MAGIC

After all the fighting they'd done against pretend zombies, Gary began to wonder what it would be like to fight *real* zombies. But he'd never seen any in Tumchester. So, he thought, if not real zombies, how about real baddies? The children had just proved how brave they could be when they rescued Marvin. With some elf magic they could become proper heroes. Or even better than that . . .

'Can you turn us into superheroes?'

The others gasped when they heard Gary say this.

'No problemo,' said Cyril. Then Bel and Ruby started clapping and laughing.

'Fantastic,' said Bel. 'Well done, Gary.'

'Galloping gooseberries,' said Ruby, giggling and bouncing on the spot.

Even Morris had to admit it was better than his doughnut idea. 'Nice one, Gary,' he said.

'Superheroes it is,' said Cyril. 'What kind do you want to be? How about I turn you into the Four Fantastic Tins of Paint? You each choose a different colour – Gary could be Green, Bel Blue, Ruby Red and Morris er, Mauve or Muddy Brown. You could have the power to paint a wall or a door or a shelf just by looking at it. In fact, I've got a spare bedroom that needs painting. You could give it a couple of coats if you fancy.'

Gary looked at Bel, who looked at Ruby, who looked at Morris, who looked at Gary. It didn't sound fantastic to them.

'I'm not sure,' said Bel politely.

'It sounds rubbish,' said Morris.

'OK,' said Cyril. 'Keep your hair on. Not tins of paint. How about you become the Four Fantastic Milkshake Kids. You are each a different flavour – Strawberry, Banana, Cabbage, Daffodil, whatever – and in times of trouble you have the power to make a lovely glass of milkshake. It'll be great. In an emergency, people will call the Milkshake Kids and you'll turn up and drink milkshakes.'

Gary said, 'So if there is a fire or a flood, we get there . . .'

'And sup, sup, sup,' said Cyril.

'I don't want to be rude,' asked Bel, 'but how will milkshakes help in an emergency?'

'It'll stop you getting thirsty!' said Cyril.

'Will we get a straw?' asked Ruby, trying to be helpful.

'A curly one,' replied Cyril, beaming.

'And we're the only people who drink these milkshakes?' asked Morris.

'Yes!' said the elf.

'OK,' said Morris, blowing out his cheeks. 'That five-headed dog trick was very clever, but now you've totally lost it.' He started walking off. 'Tins of paint. Milkshake Kids. Man's an idiot!'

'Hang on, cranky pants,' said Cyril. 'They were just ideas. I've got plenty more where they came from.'

Gary chased after Morris. 'Give him another chance,' he said, putting his arm round his friend. 'Go on.'

Morris took a deep breath. 'Fine,' he replied, 'but you do know he's off his rocker.'

The boys walked back and Gary said, 'Cyril, I don't think you understand what superheroes are. They've got brilliant special powers, like flying or being super-strong so they can lift up cars and trees.'

'Or they can go invisible,' said Bel.

'Or they have the powers of an animal, like a spider or a bat,' said Ruby.

'Hmmm. OK. I tell you what. Let's go with the animals thing,' said Cyril. He snapped his fingers and a book appeared in his hand with *Animals A to Z* written on the cover.

'Right, you each throw this book into the air. I'll chuck some elf dust at it and you'll be transformed into a fabulous superhero with the powers of whatever animal it lands on.'

'Sounds risky to me,' said Morris.

'You've got to take risks if you're going to be a superhero,' said Cyril, wisely.

Morris wasn't sure he wanted to take risks *this* big. Or, in fact, if he wanted to take any risks at all. The more he thought about it, he quite liked being normal.

'I think it sounds wicked,' said Gary.

'Me too!' said Ruby. 'I love it. Can I have the first turn? Go on. Can I?'

'It was Gary's idea so he should go first,' said Cyril, handing him the book. Gary whizzed it into the air and the elf aimed a handful of silver dust at it. There was a tiny explosion and Gary watched the book float gently on to Cyril's hand, falling open on the page that said . . .

Chimpanzee.

'Awesome!' Gary grinned, his body suddenly tingling, his muscles fizzing. Then he started jumping around. He couldn't stop himself. He leapt over Cyril's head into the branches of an oak tree and carried on climbing until he reached the top. He didn't look any different, but he felt stronger, his body was more elasticy and he was brimming with chimpanzee superpower.

'Morris, I can see your house from here,' Gary shouted. 'Yippee!' Then he started making monkey noises, somersaulting and swinging from branch to branch.

'Right. Who's next?' asked Cyril.

'Must be me, got to be, has to be!' said Ruby, but Bel's hand was up.

'Very polite, Bel,' said the elf. 'Come on, your turn.'

'Chuffin heck,' muttered Ruby.

'Thanks very much,' said Bel 'but I only wanted to ask a question. Is there a rabbit in your book? I hope not. Because I'm scared of them.'

'Can't promise there isn't,' said Cyril 'Because every species on earth is in here. But with over nine million different animals, including 950,000 insects, 28,000 fish and 10,000 birds you'd be very unlucky to get a rabbit. Just keep your fingers crossed.'

He gave her the book and Bel smiled. She threw it as high as she could, shouting, '**PLEASE DON'T LAND ON RABBIT!**' Cyril aimed his dust, there was another flash and the book opened on . . .

Nightingale.

'Woweee,' said Bel as she started to float, flapping her arms to get some direction. She looked the same, but she felt incredible. It was like being tied to a big bunch of balloons. Bel soared up past Gary in the tree and did a loop the loop. Then she hovered above Cyril's head and began to sing. Bel had always been a superb singer (she was in the school choir) – but now her voice was so powerful it shook the trees and made the ground rumble!

Bel only sang 'DO-RE-MI-FA-SO-LA-TI-DO!' but everyone had to cover their ears and Morris thought his brain was going to burst. When she'd finished they all clapped. (They were also very pleased she didn't want to sing again.) Bel flew up to join Gary in the tree.

'It must be me next isn't it? *Isn't it?*' asked Ruby, both hands in the air, jumping up and down. She couldn't stop herself. It was just so exciting.

'Of course it's you next, Ruby,' said Cyril. He gave her the book and she hurled it into the air. The elf aimed his magical dust and there was another explosion before the book landed open on . . .

Kangaroo.

'Crikey!' said Ruby, shivering with excitement. Suddenly, she started bouncing, and they were big bounces too. She bounced so high and so far she could have bounced out of the field in about three jumps.

'What's in your pocket?' asked Cyril.

Ruby had quite forgotten about kangaroos having

pouches. She found that her cardigan had grown an extra big pocket and she put her hand inside. She pulled out a toothbrush, then a trombone and then a hamster.

'It's a magic pocket,' said Cyril. 'You could pull out anything at any time.'

Ruby was delighted. She put her hand in her pocket again and pulled out a boomerang and a chicken nugget. It was marvellous. She bounced off, giggling to herself.

'OK, Morris, you're up,' said Cyril.

Morris was still having second thoughts. (Not to mention third thoughts and fourth thoughts.) He looked up to Bel and Gary in the tree. Bel waved at him and Gary gave him the thumbs up. They were having a fabulous time, chasing each other around the branches. Ruby was having fun too, laughing and bouncing down the other end of the field. Morris took a deep breath and decided to go for it.

'What are you hoping for?' asked Cyril.

'Peregrine falcon,' said Morris. He'd been learning about them at school and knew they were just about the fastest animals on the planet. 'They can fly at 264 miles an hour and that's quicker than a train,' he said proudly.

'Good choice,' said Cyril, handing him the book.

Morris hurled it into the air as he repeated,

'*Peregrine falcon, peregrine falcon, peregrine falcon
. . .*' under his breath. There was another explosion
and the book landed on Cyril's hand, open at . . .

Slug.

'Now hang on a minute!' said Morris, but as the
words were leaving his lips, his legs started twitching
and wobbling, his body got smaller and smaller, he
felt squidgier and squidgier. Soon he was the size of
a cocktail sausage and in place of his clothes was a
sluggy skin.

'**UGH!** I'm not being a slug,' he shouted, but his
voice was now very small and he sounded like when
the TV is on next door and you can just about hear it
through the wall. Morris tried to run towards Cyril, but
he found he couldn't go very fast. This was because
he didn't have any legs, just a squelchy body. He
moved forward very slowly, leaving a trail like gravy.
Morris was gutted and it was understandable.

My mum's going to
KILL me if I get home
looking like this.

SLUG FEST

Cyril crouched down next to Morris. 'Are you all right?' he asked.

'**NO I'M NOT!**' yelled Morris. 'Nobody else looks any different, only me, and they've all got great animals and mine's the worst animal ever. Change me into something else. Can't I be a peregrine falcon?'

'Sorry, old chap,' said Cyril, 'I can't turn the elf magic on and off like a tap. It chooses for itself what it thinks is best.'

Ruby bounced over, Gary swung down from the tree and Bel fluttered to a rest next to Cyril. They all looked at Morris and tried very hard not to laugh.

'It's **NOT** fair and it's **NOT** funny,' said Morris.

Cyril tried again to calm him down. 'The elf dust must have a plan for you. Can't think what it might be, though.' Cyril's eyes flicked down to the animal book, still open at the slug page. 'Look on the bright side! You now belong to a family of animals called molluscs and that means you are related to snails, oysters and giant squids.'

'I don't care what I'm related to,' said Morris. 'I've already got a mum, a dad and plenty of aunts and uncles. I don't need any squids in the family, thank you very much.'

'OK, OK. What about this,' said Cyril picking up the animal book and reading out the next interesting thing he could find. '*When in danger, slugs cover themselves in a thick slime. This makes them difficult to eat and has quite an unpleasant taste.*'

'Well, why didn't you say that in the first place?' said Morris. 'I'd completely forgotten about my ability to make slime. That makes it all better.'

Morris would have stormed off, but since he could only move very, very slowly he just squelched about a bit on the spot.

'Huddle up,' said Cyril to them all, 'and I'll explain how this superhero thing will work.' Cyril told them that their powers would only last for an hour at a time, 'Because after that you'll be pooped and you'll need to recharge the old superhero batteries'. Cyril also said they'd only become superheroes in an emergency.

'What sort of emergencies?' asked Bel.

'The kind that need superhero help,' said Cyril.

It seemed a bit vague, but the elf had done lots of amazing things in the last few minutes so they were all happy to trust him. Except Morris.

'I can't see how a slug could ever be any help to anybody ever,' he said.

'Well, you'll just have to keep your fingers crossed,' said Cyril.

'I don't have any fingers!' said Morris.

'You will in an hour,' said Cyril. 'Just cross them then. Now, before I go, we'd better choose some superhero names. Gary, let's start with you.'

'I thought about "Mr Chimpanzee",' said Gary, 'but if I had to sign any autographs I'm not sure I could spell it. So then I thought, just *The Chimp*.'

Ruby said, 'Ooh, it sounds like a pop star.'

'Lovely,' said Cyril.

Morris thought Gary was getting ahead of himself. Why would anyone want their autographs? And even if they did, Morris knew *he'd* never be able to sign any because he couldn't hold a pen. He'd have to squelch about on the page.

'Now, Bel,' said Cyril. 'I think you should simply be called *Nightingale*, don't you?'

Bel agreed. She loved her nightingale super-powers and she was thrilled with her name.

'Which means you're next, Ruby. Any thoughts?' asked the elf.

'I thought maybe *KangaRuby*,' she said.

'Great imagination,' said Cyril. 'Which means Morris you are last but . . . um . . .'

'Don't try and pretend,' said Morris. 'I know I'm least.'

Cyril said, 'We're all one big team now. So, any ideas about a name?'

'*Slug Boy,*' said Morris.

'Slug Boy?' repeated Cyril. 'Don't you want something a bit more exciting, like "The Mighty Slug" or "Captain Slug" or "Slug the Invincible" . . . ?'

'If I've got to be a slug, I'm going to be Slug Boy. I don't want to make myself sound any better than I am by using a clever name,' said Morris.

'Very noble,' said Cyril. 'So, Slug Boy, Nightingale, KangaRuby and The Chimp, let's celebrate the birth of four new superheroes and shake hands.'

'Ahem,' coughed Slug Boy, looking to where his hands would have been if he'd had any.

'Good point,' said Cyril. 'Sorry.'

So The Chimp, Nightingale, KangaRuby and Cyril shook hands and then they rubbed their fingers over Slug Boy's back for a bit.

'Last thing before I dash,' said Cyril. 'Costumes. It's sparkly leotards or all-in-one body suits normally, isn't it? Won't take me a sec.'

'Hold it right there,' said The Chimp. 'You're not dressing me up like a synchronised swimmer. We need something cool and trendy.'

'That looks nice with trainers,' said KangaRuby,

who was never out of them.

Nightingale kept quiet because she loved sparkly leotards and all-in-one body suits. Slug Boy didn't say much either since it was clear he didn't need a costume.

'Got it,' said Cyril. 'I have a fantastic eye for fashion. You want supersmart, supercool superhero costumes right?'

'Yes!' they shouted.

'Sorted!' replied the elf. 'Get a load of these babies!' He threw a last cloud of dust into the air, it exploded, and as the smoke cleared they realised they were now wearing . . . purple tracksuits, just like Cyril's. It wasn't what they were hoping for.

'Hey!' shouted The Chimp. 'You can't . . .' But Cyril was gone.

They looked more like the subs bench for a football team than a gang of superheroes, but their outfits did have a certain style. They all had masks (except Slug Boy), trainers (except Slug Boy) and KangaRuby's tracksuit top had an extra big pocket. It could have been worse. At least they weren't wearing flip flops and Viking helmets like Cyril had been.

'I miss him already,' said The Chimp.

'Me too,' said Nightingale.

'I don't,' said Slug Boy.

KangaRuby dreamily bit her fingernail. 'I thought Cyril was . . . **GROSS!**' she screamed.

'I thought you liked him,' said Nightingale. 'He gave you a magic pocket and everything.'

'**PUH! Puh–puh–puh–puh–puh!** I *did* like him!' said KangaRuby, who was blowing raspberry after raspberry. 'I can taste something horrible. On my finger. **Ugh!**'

'Ah,' said Slug Boy. 'That could've been me. Cyril's book said slugs taste totally disgusting. Some of my slime must have rubbed off on your finger when you patted me on the back. Sorry.'

'It's not your fault,' said KangaRuby, spitting into a hanky. 'And it might stop me biting my nails.'

The children spent the rest of the hour jumping, flying, climbing, bouncing and (in Slug Boy's case) wobbling about. One thing they soon learned was

37

that picking Slug Boy up was really tricky because he was slipperier than a trout in the bath.

'We'll have to figure something out,' said The Chimp, but before they could, their time was up and they were back to normal.

'I can't wait to tell the kids at school,' said Ruby as they left the field.

'I wouldn't,' warned Morris. 'Superheroes never tell anyone who they really are.'

'Oh, that's a shame,' said Ruby. 'Is it because they're shy?'

'No, it's because of the supervillains,' said Morris. 'If *they* knew who the superheroes really were they'd take revenge on their mums, dads, brothers, sisters, grandads and grandmas. Maybe even their pets.'

'I'd forgotten about the supervillains,' said Ruby. They all had. Except Morris.

'I'm sure the supervillains are all safely locked up,' said Gary, trying to make everyone feel better, although nobody quite believed him. There was an awkward silence until Ruby shoved her hand under her armpit and squeezed it so it made a trumping noise and everybody giggled. On the way home nobody chatted much. The only one with plenty to say was Marvin. He was even noisier than usual, squawking and chirruping, and he had a brand new purple feather in his tail.

38

TUMCHESTER TONIGHT

When the children got home, they all had tea and then watched *Tumchester Tonight*. It was the most popular programme in Tumchester because everyone loved the host, Dickie Trickle. He'd been the anchorman for years and was good at telling jokes as well as being serious. Dickie wore glasses with lenses like television screens and had shiny teeth to match his shiny ties.

'Good evening and welcome to *Tumchester Tonight*, with me, Dickie Trickle,' said Dickie Trickle. 'Later in the programme we find out who's got the hairiest knees in Tumchester and we meet a man who's built a wheelbarrow from fried eggs. First, we bring you shocking news, so you'd better sit down.'

Luckily, at their homes on Fish Street, Morris, Gary, Ruby and Bel were already sitting down.

Dickie Trickle carried on, 'Tumchester is in the middle of a crime wave that began this afternoon. First, the supervillain known as The Panteater escaped from prison, leaving a guard seriously in need of new pants. Twenty minutes later, he attacked again. This time it was an ice-cream seller called Harry Snettle, who has given us this exclusive interview from his hospital bed.'

The TV picture cut to a man with a red face, wrapped in a blanket. 'I was filling up my van at the petrol station when a hairy bloke asked me if I'd got ant flavour ice-cream. "Ant flavour?" I said. "Ant flavour," he said. "No," I said. "Good," he said. "It gives me tummy ache." And after that it's all a horrible blur. I woke up with a cold wind round my trousers, no pants and no ice-cream van. I'm still in shock.'

The screen switched back to Dickie shaking his head in a worried way.

'Shortly afterwards, on the other side of town, there was *another* robbery, by another supervillain. The victim was a sweet-shop owner and his attacker stole fifteen bags of sweets. Here to tell us more is the policeman in charge of the case, Detective Rigley.'

Detective Rigley had a black moustache and no hair so he looked like Mr Potato Head.

'We think we know the name of the sweet shop robber. It is this rabbit, er, pirate, er man . . . thing.' He held up a picture. 'He's called "Jumper Jack Flash" because he ties people up in their own jumpers.'

Dickie asked, 'Do you think today's crimes may be linked?'

40

'That's a good question,' replied the policeman.

'Er, so what's the answer?' asked Dickie.

'Not sure,' said Detective Rigley. 'They could be. Jumper Jack Flash and The Panteater have done all sorts of nasty things together before. They are both very dangerous and should not be approached.'

'Thank you . . .' said Dickie, shuffling his papers and turning to the camera with a concerned expression. 'Join us after the break for a wheelbarrow made of knees and the hairiest fried eggs in Tumchester. I mean, er, a wheelbarrow made of hair and some eggs with knees . . . oh, just roll the adverts!'

The news about the crime wave had been shocking indeed. Gary, Bel, Ruby and Morris were already worried about supervillains, but now they knew two of them were on the loose in Tumchester.

And one of them looks like a rabbit! thought Bel. *Oh no!*

THINGS THAT GO HOP IN THE NIGHT

Later that evening, when all the houses on Fish Street were in darkness, Jumper Jack Flash zig-zagged through the fields nearby. He stopped to sniff the air, looked around and smiled. Nobody had heard or seen anything. Then the crook set off again, his sharp rabbity teeth glinting in the moonlight. Not far from the creepy house where the children had found Mr Snuggles, there was a hedge and under it was a dark hole. This was where Jack had stashed his stolen sweets. Now he waited in the shadows for his partner.

Ten minutes later, The Panteater arrived for their secret meeting. He drove the ice-cream van slowly over the mud and reached down to turn off the headlights. But The Panteater hit the wrong button. *DIDDLY-DEE-DIDDLY-DEE-DIDDLY-DOO-DA-DOO!* the chimes started jingle-jangling and the giant ice-cream cone on the roof lit up, flashing blue and red, orange and green.

'No! No!' screamed The Panteater, his fingers

42

moving over the dashboard like disco-dancing spiders. 'Where's the button, where's the button?!'

DIDDLY-DEE-DIDDLY-DEE-DIDDLY-DOO-DA-DOO! the chimes carried on ringing out noisily.

'Shut up, shut up, shut up! AAAGGGHHH!' he yelled until, at last, he found the button for the chimes. He wiped the sweat from his hairy brow and looked over at the houses on Fish Street. There wasn't even a twitchy curtain. He took another deep breath and parked by the hole.

Seconds later there was a tap at the van window and Jumper Jack Flash's one eye stared in. The Panteater opened the door.

'I'm sure you could have tried a bit harder to draw attention to yourself,' said Jumper Jack. 'Why didn't you hire some geese to march in front of the van and put some clowns on the roof singing karaoke?'

'It wasn't my fault,' fibbed The Panteater. 'And anyway, nobody saw me.'

Jumper Jack Flash narrowed his eye suspiciously. 'Good job,' he said. 'Now help me with the bags.'

After the stolen sweets were loaded on to the van the crooks drove off into the night. They headed north for a long time until they stopped at an old funfair on the edge of town.

Fluffy's Funfair had closed down years before and the huge rusty gates at the front were padlocked.

43

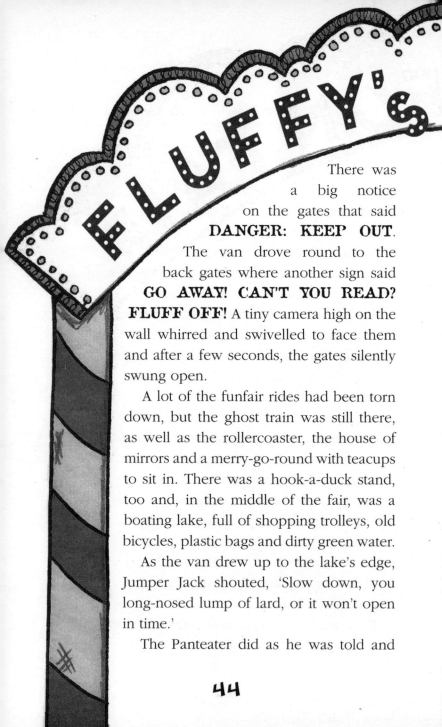

There was a big notice on the gates that said **DANGER: KEEP OUT**. The van drove round to the back gates where another sign said **GO AWAY! CAN'T YOU READ? FLUFF OFF!** A tiny camera high on the wall whirred and swivelled to face them and after a few seconds, the gates silently swung open.

A lot of the funfair rides had been torn down, but the ghost train was still there, as well as the rollercoaster, the house of mirrors and a merry-go-round with teacups to sit in. There was a hook-a-duck stand, too and, in the middle of the fair, was a boating lake, full of shopping trolleys, old bicycles, plastic bags and dirty green water.

As the van drew up to the lake's edge, Jumper Jack shouted, 'Slow down, you long-nosed lump of lard, or it won't open in time.'

The Panteater did as he was told and

44

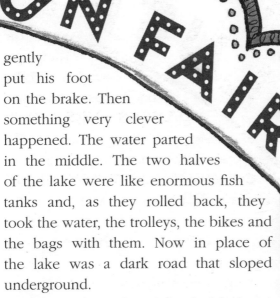

gently
put his foot
on the brake. Then
something very clever
happened. The water parted
in the middle. The two halves
of the lake were like enormous fish
tanks and, as they rolled back, they
took the water, the trolleys, the bikes and
the bags with them. Now in place of
the lake was a dark road that sloped
underground.

The van drove down into the blackness
and stopped at the bottom where The
Panteater flicked a switch on the wall,
sliding the lake back into place. Then
the crooks drove down a twisting tunnel,
their headlights picking out the eyeballs
of frogs and rats lurking in the shadows
as green water trickled down the walls. At
last the van stopped at an iron door that
rose up to let them in.

This was the warehouse and inside
robot mice were waiting to unload the

45

stolen sweets. The mice were the size of grown men and they didn't speak (they didn't even squeak).

'Those guys give me the creeps,' whispered The Panteater.

'Me too,' replied Jack. 'But if they weren't here, guess who'd be the ones breaking their backs getting the stuff off the van?'

'Oh, I love a quiz,' said The Panteater. 'Can I phone a friend?'

'No, you hairbrain!' said Jack. 'You haven't got a phone. Or any friends. Except me. And I know the answer.'

'OK, is it vegetable, animal or mineral?' asked The Panteater.

'It's not a quiz!' said Jack. '*We'd* be doing it! Us! You and me!'

'I knew that,' said The Panteater. 'I was pretending not to know because I thought you didn't know.'

'Come on, or we'll be late,' said Jack, shaking his head.

The supervillains left the warehouse and took a lift down to a beautiful office where chandeliers hung like diamond necklaces and the carpet was thick, red velvet. In a corner was an enormous aquarium full of pink blobby things that swayed and swished. A sign on the front said:

RASPBERRY JELLYFISH: VERY VERY HIGHLY DANGEROUS

46

At the end of the office was a desk and behind it was a dark figure sitting in a swivel chair. He didn't turn round to face his guests.

'Good to have you out of prison, Panteater,' he said. 'I assume my plan worked perfectly.'

'It did, Boss,' replied The Panteater, licking his lips as he remembered the prison guard's pants.

'And how was your raid on the sweet shop, Jack?'

'Mission accomplished, Boss,' said Jumper Jack.

'Not quite mission accomplished,' said The Boss. 'It's just the end of the beginning . . . of the end!' And the sound of his laughter was like water going down a plughole. 'Hlug, hlug, hlug, hlug.'

THINGS THEY DIDN'T KNOW THEY DIDN'T KNOW

The next day was Saturday. At 27 Fish Street, Gary spent the morning looking up facts about chimpanzees on his computer, printing off pictures and sticking them on the wall in place of his football posters. His dad walked in.

'What you up to, our Gaz?' he asked.

'Nothing,' said Gary, who wanted to get on with his chimp research.

'I can see it's something,' replied his dad. 'Have you gone off Tumchester United and started supporting the ugliest football team in the world? It's not Tumchester City is it?'

'It's homework,' said Gary. 'We've got to learn about chimpanzees.'

'Oh,' said his dad, looking at a picture of a big, hairy chimp in a cowboy hat. 'That reminds me, your mother's out line-dancing again tonight so you'll have to stay here.'

Gary's mum and dad didn't live together so Gary and his younger sister, Nancy, were always going

48

backwards and forwards between them.

'I've learnt all sorts of great stuff about chimps,' said Gary. 'Did you know they are highly intelligent?'

'I wouldn't say *highly* intelligent,' laughed his dad. 'I've never seen one do a Sudoku.'

'You're not funny, Dad,' said Gary. 'They kiss just like people and they use tools as well, like putting sticks down holes to get ants out to eat.'

'Use tools do they?' said his dad. 'See if you can get one to fix my car. It'd be a lot cheaper than the garage.'

Gary tried not to smile but he couldn't help it. His dad's jokes were so unfunny they somehow ended up funny.

'Look, I'd love to talk chimps all day, but your lunch is ready,' said Dad.

'OK, I'll be down in five minutes,' said Gary, hoping it was bananas and custard for pudding.

A few houses away, at 33 Fish Street, Bel was sitting on her bed with Cuddles, her cat. She'd found out all she could about nightingales and was filling up a little notebook in her best handwriting. Amongst other things, Bel learned that:

Nightingales love to sing both day and night, while most birds only sing in the day.

(Bel felt this was great news because sometimes she might have to fight supervillains in the dark.)

In the summer, many nightingales fly to South Africa.

(Bel always went to Skegness and stayed in a caravan so South Africa sounded very exciting.)

The most famous of all nightingales is Florence Nightingale, who wasn't actually a bird. She was a nurse who looked after wounded soldiers.

(Bel loved the thought that she was following in Florence's footsteps helping people and maybe even saving lives.)

'Bel, it's lunch time,' whispered her mum from the door. 'I've boiled your egg for exactly three minutes thirty-six and a half seconds, just as you like it.' Bel's parents were nice, but a bit too fussy so Bel had to be really patient with them.

'Thanks, Mum!' she answered. 'By the way, are we still going to Skegness this year? Because I've got another idea. Can we go to South Africa?'

'Princess!' said her mum seriously. 'You know we can't go somewhere like that.'

'Oh yes,' said Bel. 'Sorry, I forgot. You and Dad are scared of flying.'

'Terrified is the word, darling,' said her mum. 'If we were meant to fly we'd have wings. But we aren't, so we don't.'

Bel wondered what her Mum would say if she'd

seen her daughter soaring through the sky and looping the loop last night. She chuckled to herself.

Ruby was in the living room at 36 Fish Street, sitting under a pile of books about Australia she'd got from the library. She learned lots of useful kangaroo information, such as how fast they could hop and how high, but Ruby's favourite fact was . . .

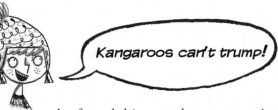

Kangaroos can't trump!

As soon as she found this out, she ran upstairs to tell her gran who nearly fell off the bed laughing.

'Jumping jellybeans!' she chuckled. 'Not even after brussel sprouts, beans on toast and chicken curry?'

'I don't think so,' said Ruby, giggling too.

'I wish I knew their secret,' said her gran. 'Last night, my trumps were so noisy your dad thought there must be fireworks outside. He kept dashing into the garden to look for them!'

Ruby laughed. 'The whiff nearly knocked Marvin off his perch! Poor thing. He didn't squawk for hours.'

At 61 Fish Street Morris had decided to stay in bed for as long as he could and forget about the whole superhero business. When he finally got up, he wandered into the garden where his dad was cutting the grass and his mum was kneeling in the flowerbed. He noticed his mum had a beaker full of dead slugs in her hand and they seemed to be floating in a sea of sour milk.

'What you doing?' asked Morris. Whatever it was, it didn't look good for the slugs.

'Slugs,' she murmured. 'I hate them. Slimy and horrible. Always making great big holes in my lettuces.'

'How come you've got a cup full?' asked Morris, mystified.

'This is a slug trap,' said Morris's mum. 'I fill it with milk and bury it in the ground so you can just see the top. Then I wait. The slugs come out at night and guzzle it down. But they can't stop, they're all having such a good time they drink too much and drown.'

Morris thought that slugs couldn't be too clever if *that* caught them out. Still, no need to drown them for it. 'Sounds cruel to me,' he said, staring at the little creatures.

'There's nothing wrong with being nasty to slugs,' said his mum. 'Sometimes I sprinkle them with salt and watch them fizzle to death. It's better than the telly.'

Suddenly Morris was feeling very sorry for slugs. It wasn't their fault they liked a nice bit of salad.

VOWS ON SUNDAY

A cold wind rattled through the city, carrying the clanging sound of the church bells far over Tumchester. Ruby was struggling on her paper round. The Sunday papers were as heavy as gravestones and the gale was making her job impossible. She had other things on her mind too. Marvin was off his food. He hadn't been the same since they'd met Cyril and she was worried that all the elf magic had scared him a bit silly.

When Ruby had finished her paper round, she rode her bike over to Bel's house for a meeting with Gary, Bel and Morris. They always went there when they had something important to talk about because it was so quiet. Even when Bel's mum and dad were shouting it sounded like they were whispering, and their hobby was listening to classical music with the volume on low.

When Ruby walked in, she was happy to find that so far they'd only been talking about the end-of-term prom. But soon they got on to the topic they really,

really wanted to discuss: being superheroes.

'We should make a vow,' said Gary thoughtfully.

'Fantastic idea! I can't wait. I've always wanted to make a vow,' said Ruby. 'But I'm not totally sure what one is.'

'It's like a promise,' said Bel. 'One you can't ever break. People say vows when they get married.'

'That's right!' said Ruby. She put on a deep voice. 'I vow to love you and be your awful wedded wife.' They all giggled.

'We should vow to fight for good and never use our special powers for evil,' said Gary.

'Do we have to?' said Morris.

'Yes,' said the other three together.

So they stood in a circle and Ruby and Bel said they should hold hands, but the boys felt awkward. Morris pulled the sleeve of his jumper down so that Bel and Ruby weren't actually holding his hand and Gary said, 'I don't think I've ever seen any other superheroes holding hands.' So they all ended up putting their hands in the middle. Then they took their vow to fight for good and never use their powers for evil.

Afterwards Gary picked up a glass of lemonade and said, 'Let's drink a toast to us, The Fish Fingers!'

'Hang on,' said Morris. 'The Fish Fingers doesn't sound quite superhero-ey enough to me. It was all right when we were only kids playing but . . .'

'It just needs beefing up!' said Ruby. 'Let's be The Fiery Four Fish Fingers of Fury!'

'Bit of a mouthful,' said Morris.

Ruby tried something else. 'The Furious Fists of Fingers and Famous Fish?'

'Sounds like a kung fu film,' said Morris.

'Or something you'd have with egg-fried rice,' said Gary.

Then Bel said, 'How about The Fabulous Four Fish Fingers?'

'That's it!' cried Gary and the others agreed. Even Morris liked it. They chinked their lemonade and cheered.

SHOPS AND ROBBERS

The next day, straight after school, Gary, Bel, Ruby and Morris went shopping at the Tumchester mall. It was one of their favourite places because it was full of sweet smells, dazzling displays and people giving away free stuff like perfume, chocolate or cheese.

The children were in a shop called *Kool 4 Kidz* searching for trendy clothes to wear to the end of term prom. It was the biggest night in the school calendar and it was only two weeks away. Gary soon picked out a pair of skinny jeans, Bel found some trainers with gold stripes and Ruby was trying on a baseball cap with glittery stars on. Morris was looking at himself in some sunglasses when he heard a voice he knew only too well.

'Hello Doris!' shouted Charlie Snodgrass, a boy with crooked teeth, muscles like a bag of oranges and tiger-skin socks. Everybody called him Snoddy. At his shoulder was Peter Ferret, who had slicked back hair and a neck full of gold chains.

'Yeah, hello Doris, huh huh huh huh,' said Ferret, who wasn't the sharpest crayon in the pencil case.

Luckily, Gary saw what was happening and he dashed to Morris's rescue. 'Clear off you two,' he said. 'We get enough of you at school.'

But Snoddy ignored him, pinched Morris's ear and gave it a twist.

Morris squealed, '*OW!*'

Ruby and Bel crowded round Morris like big sisters. Gary shoved Snoddy against a shelf of jumpers.

'I told you to get lost,' Gary warned.

Snoddy shook his head. 'You puzzle me, Gary,' he said. 'I can't understand why somebody like you hangs around with a loser like Doris AND two girls.'

'Maybe Gary likes us because we are nice to people,' said Ruby.

'Hush, little girl. Big boys are talking,' said Snoddy. 'Go and try on some shoes or something.'

Gary stared at him. Much as he hated Snoddy, there was something sort of cool about him too, especially his tiger-skin socks. Gary backed down.

'Just chill out,' he said, but then Ferret saw a chance to prove he was as tough as Snoddy.

'Wanna start something?' he hissed, grabbing Gary by his shirt. At that moment another face from school appeared in the shop window. It was Mr Jolly, their teacher.

'Hello boys and girls,' he said, coming through the door. 'Anything the matter?'

Mr Jolly was wearing the same beige suit that he wore every day, with a beige shirt, beige shoes and a beige tie. His hair was like a blob of vanilla ice cream. Although he'd been at Fish Street School for less than a year, Mr Jolly was already very popular.

Ferret let Gary go when he saw Mr Jolly.

'I think Charles and Peter were looking for something, but it's not here,' said Bel.

Yeah, they were looking for trouble, thought Morris.

'They're just leaving,' said Gary.

'Oh well,' said Mr Jolly. 'No doubt they are rushing off to practise their spellings for our test.'

'Yeah,' said Snoddy. 'We are.' But as he left he whispered into Morris's ear, 'Don't bother bringing a packed lunch tomorrow, because you'll be getting knuckle sandwiches from me.'

Ferret followed him out, making an 'L' shape with his thumb and his finger then pointing at Morris.

'Good riddance,' said Bel.

Mr Jolly polished his glasses with a little black hanky and smiled at the Fish Fingers. 'See you at school,' he said and headed off towards the escalators.

'He's lovely, don't you think?' said Ruby. 'Like a knight in beige armour.'

The others all agreed.

Meanwhile in the mall car park, Jumper Jack Flash and The Panteater had just pulled up in their ice-cream van. Wanted posters with their faces on were all over town so they'd disguised themselves as chickens and they were covered from head to toe in hundreds of yellow feathers.

From the back of the van they unloaded a giant shopping trolley with two rocket-shaped fireworks stuck to the sides and headed straight to the sweet aisle of the supermarket. They started piling their trolley high with goodies and a little crowd soon gathered.

Everyone laughed at the cute, fluffy chickens. They didn't understand it was a robbery. Not until Jumper Jack Flash said in a loud voice, 'This is a robbery.'

A tall security guard stepped forward, 'Oh no you don't,' he said. 'Or . . .'

No one ever found out what the guard was going to say next. With electrifying speed, Jumper Jack leapt into the air and kicked the man twenty times in a hundred different places. (It was so fast it could have been a hundred times in twenty places. It was definitely lots of times, in lots of places.) Then the villain wrapped his victim up so tight in his jumper sleeves he could have rolled him out of the shop like a bowling ball.

'Nobody else move,' shouted The Panteater. 'Or you'll pay with your pants.'

Somebody did move. It was Snoddy. He'd seen a few fruit gums drop on the floor and he bent down to shove them in his pocket. The Panteater saw. The villain grabbed Snoddy with his huge claws, held the boy above his head, then slurped up his pants like a glass of grape juice.

Snoddy screamed, '*EEEEEEUUUUGGGGH!!!*'

The Panteater burped.

Over at *Kool 4 Kidz* the Fabulous Four Fish Fingers started to feel their bodies tingle and their clothes morph into their superhero outfits. Within seconds, Tumchester's newest, nicest crime fighters were racing off to save the day. At least they would have been, if things hadn't gone disastrously wrong.

The Chimp was in a fitting room trying on his new jeans. In the excitement he put both feet into one trouser leg, jumped up, tripped over, banged his head on the door and gave himself a nosebleed. He had to sit on a stool for the next ten minutes, pinching his nose to stop the blood.

Nightingale didn't get much further. She was in such a flutter she flew straight into the plate glass door of *Kool 4 Kidz*. She stumbled out of the exit, setting off the security alarms because she was still carrying one of the trainers she'd picked out for the prom. A store detective caught her by the arm shouting, 'Shoplifter, shoplifter! Call the police! You'll be locked up for this!' and he frogmarched her back inside.

Slug Boy was in a grumpy mood from the start. *Just what I don't need*, he thought. *A proper emergency.* He wobbled and shrank and sat behind a sock display waiting for one of the others to pick him up. KangaRuby did, but he squirted out of her hand so fast and so far she had no idea where he went. She gave up looking and dashed out on her own. Then she stopped. What should she do now? Without the others, KangaRuby hadn't got a clue.

At the supermarket, the villains had filled their trolley and Jumper Jack now lit the rockets on the side. They exploded with a whizz and a

FWEEEEEEEEEEEEEE*!*

The shopping trolley zoomed off, knocking over people, plant pots and a pyramid of pineapples. Jumper Jack Flash and The Panteater dashed after it, hooting and brushing away security guards as if they were flecks of dandruff.

'It's going like *cluck*-work!' shouted The Panteater, as they smashed through the supermarket doors, leaving a trail of yellow feathers behind them.

'The *yolk*'s on them!' crowed Jack. 'Cock-a-doodle-**DOOOOOOOOOOOOOOOO!**'

KangaRuby was waiting nervously outside *Kool 4 Kidz* and as the crooks got nearer, she thrust her hand into her magic pocket and pulled out . . .

A bunch of tulips. As the villains sped past it looked like she was waving them off.

The Panteater waved back. *Must be a fan*, he

thought. *With my good looks I'm surprised there aren't a few more.*

As he reached the exit, The Panteater saw KangaRuby was still fishing in her pocket. *Bet she's looking for an autograph book*, he thought, giving her another wave. Then the chickens crossed the road, jumped into their van and screeched out of the car park.

Full of gloom, KangaRuby trudged back to *Kool 4 Kidz*. She found The Chimp with his head between his knees in the fitting room. Then she tracked down Nightingale who'd been left in a back office by the security guard while he went to see what was happening outside. They all searched high and low for Slug Boy until Nightingale found him splatted to the window. None of the Fish Fingers felt fabulous at all.

TIME FOR TRICKLE

Later on, long after they'd changed back to normal, the Fish Fingers sat down to watch *Tumchester Tonight* at Ruby's house. Of course, the robbery was the big story and there was even a shot of Snoddy. The anchorman Dickie Trickle described Snoddy as a 'poor innocent victim who'd lost his pants'.

Afterwards, Detective Rigley was interviewed in the studio again.

'My officers have been working on this twenty-four hours a day and sometimes even more than that. It is now clear Jumper Jack Flash and The Panteater have joined forces,' he said.

'Have you any advice for the public?' asked Dickie.

'Yes. The crooks were last seen disguised as chickens so please be careful when you approach any chickens, even if they are covered in gravy on plates with carrots and peas.'

'Are you saying the villains could be disguised as a Sunday roast?' asked Dickie.

'Yes and no,' said the Detective.

'Yes?' asked Dickie.

'No,' said Rigley. 'But they are highly dangerous and should not be tackled, except by trained police officers.'

'Thank you,' said Dickie Trickle. 'I hope you'll let us know if there is any more *fowl* play.' He chuckled at his own joke, but the policeman didn't find it funny. Then the man who reads the sports news came on.

At the old deserted funfair on the edge of town, The Boss turned the TV off.

'What did you do that for?' complained The Panteater. 'There's a very interesting report on hedgehogs playing badminton next.'

'We've got more important things to think about,' said The Boss.

'The police?' asked Jumper Jack.

'Not the police,' said The Boss. 'They couldn't catch a number 47 bus, let alone a gang of criminal masterminds like us.'

The Panteater licked some wax out of his ear with his tongue as Jumper Jack picked an old marshmallow off the bottom of his foot and ate it.

'Make that criminal masterminds like *some* of us,' murmured The Boss under his breath,

The Boss always wore dark sunglasses and he dressed head to foot in black. He wore a black shirt, black shoes, black socks, black tie and black trousers. He even wore black swimming trunks when he went swimming. He wished he had black hair as well, but his hair was ginger. When he was younger he tried wearing clothes to match the colour of his hair, but with orange shoes, orange socks, orange trousers and an orange shirt he looked like a satsuma. This combination is no good if you want to make people shake with fear. Nobody is afraid of satsumas, even ones with an evil laugh. So black clothes it was, even if it didn't match his hair.

'Come on,' said The Boss to his henchmen. 'I've got big plans for you two and the sooner we get on with things, the better.'

At 36 Fish Street it was time for Ruby's tea and the other Fish Fingers had to go home. They all gave Marvin a wave before they left, but the parrot was still down in the dumps. He gave them a little whistle and a quick 'MAAARVIN'S STAAARVIN' but he clearly wasn't himself.

'The only thing he'll eat at the moment is salt-and-vinegar crisps. I don't know what's come over him,' Ruby whispered.

Ruby thought she might have to take him to the vets, but in actual fact there was nobody on Earth who could help Marvin. That was because Marvin wasn't actually on Earth. He was having a wonderful holiday in the elf world and it was Cyril who was living in Marvin's cage.

When Cyril turned the children into superheroes, he decided to change places with Marvin for a while to keep an eye on them. The trouble was the elf had now forgotten how to un-parrot himself. He was always quite scatter-brained, but this was the biggest mess he had ever got into. He couldn't talk (except to say 'MAAARVIN'S STAAARVIN') and he couldn't use his elf magic! All he could do was look in Marvin's mirror, ring his little bell and hope to remember.

Cyril knew that if he didn't think of the un-parrot spell soon, he'd be no use to anyone and stuck inside a cage for the rest of his days. And, since most elves lived to be 999 and he was only 463, that was a lot of days. Poor Cyril. No wonder he was feeling grumpy.

MORRIS DANCING

It was the morning after the raid on the supermarket and at Fish Street School rumours about Snoddy were bouncing off the walls. As Gary, Bel, Ruby and Morris filed out of their classroom and trudged across the playground to the school hall the stories got bigger and bigger.

'He's getting an Olympic medal for bravery,' said one boy.

'Snoddy works undercover for the police. He has done for years,' whispered another.

A girl said, 'Did you know Snoddy ate The Panteater's own pants to save someone's life.'

'It was the Queen's life,' chipped in someone else. 'She was at the supermarket buying some jewels.'

'There was a two-for-one jewel sale on,' said one boy. 'Even the Queen likes a bargain. Snoddy's her personal shopper – he picks out all her bling.'

The headteacher, Mrs Pompidoor, had asked Snoddy to say a few words in assembly. Mrs Pompidoor was a large woman with tiny, round glasses and a beaky nose that made her look like a woodpigeon. She stood on the stage next to Snoddy, clapping everything he said.

'With the store guard down, I knew I was the only one who could stop those crooks,' said Snoddy. 'So, first of all, I karate chopped the rabbity one, Jumper Jack Flash. We had a big karate fight and I won, but he escaped. Then I grabbed the big, hairy one, The Panteater. I wrestled him to the ground and I could have beaten him, even though he was as big as a telephone box. But he fought dirty. He picked me up and . . . and . . . I don't want to say what happened next.'

'Of course, Charles,' said Mrs Pompidoor, wiping tears from her eyes. 'You were such a hero. Let's give this brave boy a big clap everybody.'

There was a huge round of applause and Snoddy grinned. Then Mrs Pompidoor made an announcement. 'We will be holding the final auditions for the prom night talent show here in the hall straight after assembly. Stay back if you got through the first round.'

Most of the children trooped off, but about twenty waited behind. This group included Gary, Bel, Ruby, Morris, Snoddy and Ferret.

'Be with you in a moment,' shouted Mrs Pompidoor, leaving the hall to get a clipboard. As soon as she'd gone, Snoddy gave Morris a Chinese burn, twisting the skin on his arm two ways at the same time.

'**Owwww!** What's that for?' yelled Morris.

'Because I can,' said Snoddy.

'Well, don't,' answered Morris.

'You should treat heroes with more respect,' sneered Ferret.

Morris took a swipe at Snoddy and missed just as Mrs Pompidoor came back into the hall.

'Morris!' she shouted. 'I hope you aren't being unkind to our hero.'

'No, Mrs Pompidoor,' he answered. But he was thinking *very* unkind thoughts.

Only five acts would make it through to the final of the talent show and Mrs Pompidoor was going to be judging along with Mr Jolly and Miss Diddle (the drama teacher who wore orange lipstick and purple nail varnish). Miss Diddle soon arrived, but Mr Jolly didn't.

'Mr Jolly has had to take his cat to the vets,' announced Mrs Pompidoor. 'So he sends a big sorry and wishes you all good luck.'

Ruby was especially disappointed, although she hoped his cat would be all right.

The children all sat in front of the stage, waiting to go on. Most were going to sing (including Morris and Bel), but there were lots of novelty acts too like acrobats and magicians. Gary was going to juggle a football, Ruby was going to tap dance and Snoddy and Ferret were going to do a rap.

After an hour the judges had seen all the acts except Morris and he figured there was probably just one place left in the show. Bel and Ruby had both been terrific so they were definitely in. Gary had dropped his ball a few times so he was probably out. Snoddy and Ferret had been rubbish, but Mrs Pompidoor kept smiling at her 'hero' so they were probably in, along with a brilliant violinist called Lionel.

As for the rest . . . one of the acrobats cartwheeled off stage and landed headfirst in the piano. A 'Crazy Cream Cracker Eater' only managed to eat two crackers before he was sick all over Miss Diddle. (He was later found to have eaten seventeen packets backstage for practice.) A magician failed to pull a mouse out of her hat after it got stuck down the back of her shirt and a boy playing 'Happy Birthday' on the mouth organ got so excited he swallowed his own instrument.

Morris knew he could take the last spot if he sang well. He handed his backing CD to the girl in charge of the music and stepped onto the stage. The spotlight came on and the first few notes began. Morris gripped the microphone tightly. He opened his mouth and . . .

WhFFFrrrrrrrrrrrrrrrr . . .

'Pardon?' said Mrs Pompidoor.
'Is that part of the song?'

Whhoooooaaarpp . . .

It was happening! Morris was
turning into Slug Boy on stage, in
front of everyone and there was
nothing he could do to stop it. If he changed now,
his secret would be out. His legs were twitching like
two haddocks on a fishing line.

'Is he dancing?' Mrs Pompidoor asked the teacher
next to her. 'Or feeling a bit funny?'

Miss Diddle wasn't sure.

Nnnnnnnnnnnnnnnnn!

Morris tried to run but his legs
were wobbling and twisting so
much he fell flat on the floor.

'Are they your best moves, Doris?' laughed Snoddy. Everybody started giggling except for Gary, Bel and Ruby, but they didn't know how to help. At any second Morris would transform into Slug Boy and the Fish Fingers would be as good as over! Ruby bit her nails. Gary held his breath. Bel shut her eyes.

Just then, a boy burst through the doors and screamed.

'It ate my p-pants.'

Everybody turned round to look and at that exact moment, Morris shrank into Slug Boy.

THE BATTLE OF FISH STREET SCHOOL

'I-it ate my p-p-pants,' the boy said again. 'And it's still in there, somewhere.'

'It ate your pants and it's still in your pants?' asked Mrs Pompidoor, baffled.

'No!' said the boy. 'It's in the school. The hairy robber, from the TV. They're both here – the one-eyed rabbit as well. They broke into the tuck shop and now they're taking everybody's sweets.'

At last Mrs Pompidoor understood. This was an emergency! She turned back to the children auditioning.

'Everybody wait here while I investigate.'

She didn't notice that four key contestants had already left. (And she didn't see her brave hero Snoddy cowering in the costume cupboard either.)

KangaRuby bounced, Nightingale soared and The Chimp swung with Slug Boy gripped in his fingers towards the main building. The scene that greeted them was truly terrible. Dozens of children were lying in the playground, tied up in their own jumpers,

74

groaning, crying and rolling around. Others were staggering out of classrooms, quivering with shock. The Chimp stopped to ask a girl leaning against a wall where the crooks had gone.

'The Arts block,' said the girl breathlessly. 'I-I saw them on the fourth floor.'

'Thanks,' said The Chimp. 'And don't worry – we're here to save you.'

The girl smiled, even though she couldn't quite remember which emergency service it was that wore masks and purple tracksuits.

Slug Boy shouted to The Chimp. 'What do you mean "We're here to save you"? *How* exactly? We're just kids! And, if it all goes wrong, who is going to save me – I mean – us?'

But nobody heard him because they weren't really listening. Besides, he was very muffled inside The Chimp's hand.

Soon the Fabulous Four Fish Fingers reached the Arts block and The Chimp took command. 'You're up first, Nightingale. Do a quick spot check from the outside. Tell us what you can see.'

But Nightingale was jittery.

'Hang on,' she said. 'I'm not sure I can do this.' For someone who hated even cute little bunnies, the thought of meeting a one-eyed robber rabbit was the stuff of nightmares.

'Don't be such a girl,' said The Chimp, which wasn't very helpful.

'Just try,' said KangaRuby gently.

Nightingale took a deep breath and rocketed into the sky, hovering outside the classroom windows on the fourth floor. Her stomach turned over. She could see the two villains laughing as another class of children emptied their pockets and put all their sweets into a huge, bulging bag. Nightingale flew back down.

'It's them,' she said. 'The hairy one and the r-r-r-rabbit. They're moving from class to class.'

'Got it,' said KangaRuby. 'That means they'll come back this way or go down the stairs by Mr Jolly's classroom.'

The Chimp spotted a small open window on the fourth floor.

'OK,' he said. 'I'll go up the drainpipe and climb into the classrooms. Then I'll get them to chase me down the stairs. You two wait at the bottom and catch them there.'

Just then The Chimp remembered Slug Boy in his hand. He opened his fingers.

'About time somebody thought about me,' said Slug Boy in a huff.

'Sorry,' said The Chimp. 'Er, you'd better just hang on here. It's safer.' He put his friend on the ground and covered him over with a plant pot. Then he leapt onto the drainpipe and nimbly climbed up it. KangaRuby bounced and Nightingale flew to find the stairs.

'Flipping charming,' said Slug Boy, although because he was under the plant pot it sounded like 'ffffpig chrmmmmig.'

The Chimp climbed to the top of the drainpipe in seconds and somersaulted through the open window to land neatly on his feet. The classroom was empty, but screams came from the room next door as a crowd of children ran off. The Chimp grabbed two handfuls from a heap of wet modelling clay and peered round the corner. The Panteater and Jumper Jack Flash were holding a boy upside down so that the toffees in his pocket dropped onto the floor.

Taking careful aim, The Chimp threw the clay.

SPLaT!

The first ball went so far up The Panteater's nose it almost came out of his ears.

PHWaT!

The other ball hit Jumper Jack's one good eye.

'*WHAAAAAAAAA!*' shouted the rabbit, staggering into a pile of chairs. As The Panteater angrily licked his nose clean and Jack wiped the clay from his face, The Chimp whooped like a monkey. He snatched up the toffees and yelled, 'Catch me if you can, losers!'

11

The villains looked up as The Chimp leapt for the light that hung from the ceiling and swung into the corridor, The Panteater's claw swiping the air behind him.

Meanwhile, KangaRuby and Nightingale reached the bottom of the staircase. It was a great place for a trap because at the bottom there was a swing door. They decided to hide behind it, then jump out.

'Right, let's see what we've got in this pocket,' said KangaRuby, dipping her hand in and pulling out a lettuce. 'Sorry.' Then a garden gnome. 'Whoops.' Then a hairdryer. 'Sorry, again.'

'It's not much good so far,' said Nightingale anxiously, thinking about the rabbit.

'I can't help it,' tutted KangaRuby. 'I never know what's coming out. One last go.'

This time she pulled out a pole with a huge fishing net on the end.

'Perfect,' said Nightingale, who took hold of it and flew up to the top of the door, where she hovered out of sight.

Upstairs, The Chimp was running out of breath. He managed to dodge and shimmy in between the two villains, but they were tough and strong. As The Chimp jumped from the top of a tall bookcase, Jumper Jack leapt too, swinging his foot and catching The Chimp in his tummy. Gasping for breath, The

Chimp rolled over just as The Panteater's long tongue slithered out to make a meal of his pants. He ran towards the stairs and bounded down three at a time, but the villains were close and catching.

'**HERE THEY COME!**' The Chimp yelled.

Nightingale saw the door swing open and swung the net down . . . on top of The Chimp.

'Help!' he howled and Nightingale dropped the net in surprise. But that made it worse – the more he struggled, the more he tangled himself up. Nightingale tried to get him out. 'But you said "*Here they come!*' she explained.

'Yes,' shouted The Chimp. 'Here they come, **AFTER ME!**'

Then Jumper Jack Flash and The Panteater burst through the door. With the Chimp and Nightingale tied up, everything depended on KangaRuby.

'Stop where you are or I'll hit you with **THIS!**' she shouted, pulling a pair of socks from her pocket.

'Not those, **THIS!**'

It was a comb. 'Oh dear. How about **THIS?**'

A slice of toast.

The crooks looked at each other and giggled. KangaRuby was all flustered. She rummaged around in her pocket, but her fingers felt like lumps of concrete. Jumper Jack ducked down low and swung his leg so that it tripped KangaRuby and she fell backwards, straight into the net, with The Chimp.

Next, Jumper Jack turned to Nightingale. He moved slowly towards her, like a shark swimming towards lunch. Nightingale closed her eyes and when she opened them again the villain was so close she could feel his breath on her face. It was too much. She leapt into the air and flapped off towards a clump of trees on the school field and there she sat, trying not to think about rabbits.

'Time to leg it,' said Jumper Jack.

'Couldn't I just grab another pair of pants?' said The Panteater. 'I'm still peckish.'

'You'll spoil your tea,' answered his partner. 'And you always get itchy gums when you eat too many. Let's go, before the police turn up.'

The Panteater sighed. 'It's like doing robberies with my mum. I'm surprised you're not telling me to wear a vest.'

'If the police get here we'll both be *under a-vest!*' snapped Jack.

The Panteater looked confused.

'A-*vest* . . . like *arrest* . . . Oh, never mind,' sighed Jack. 'Let's scarper!' They picked up their bags of stolen sweets and ran to the ice-cream van. With a screech of tyres, they were gone.

Back by the stairs, KangaRuby and The Chimp untangled themselves from the fishing net and

Nightingale fluttered down from the tree into the school.

'Right, let's get after them,' said KangaRuby and she leapt into the air, but her feet hardly left the ground.

'I think our hour is up,' said Morris walking round the corner. 'And thank you all very much for making me feel a huge part of the team. You can be The Three Fish Fingers from now on. I won't be joining in again. Ever.'

'Sorry, Mozz. It was my fault,' said Gary. 'It won't happen again.'

'Too right it won't,' said Morris. 'Because next time I'll be sitting at home watching telly or taking the dog for a walk.'

'You haven't got a dog,' said Ruby. 'But you could take Marvin for a walk I suppose, or Bel's cat. He'll leave cat hairs on your jumper, though.'

'You're not helping,' said Morris.

'If Morris is leaving, so am I,' said Bel. 'Nobody said there'd be an emergency with a rabbit in it.'

'Fine. Count me out too,' said Gary. 'Girls are rubbish superheroes anyway. I'm going to team up with Snoddy.'

The other three stared at him. It was almost as bad as saying he was joining Jumper Jack Flash and The Panteater. Gary hadn't really meant it but now he'd said it he wasn't taking it back. Suddenly there was only one superhero left.

'Right. Well, I'm not doing it on my own,' said Ruby. 'The Fabulous One Fish Finger sounds silly.' So then there were none.

Gloomily, they headed round to the front of the school where teachers, pupils, dinner ladies and the caretaker were milling about. Children who'd been tied up in their jumpers were being unwrapped and the ones who'd been attacked by The Panteater were sipping hot orange squash.

Later on the police arrived and started asking questions. Nobody could figure out how the crooks had got in because the school gates hadn't been smashed and the locks hadn't been broken. At one o'clock, the headteacher gave everybody the rest of the day off. Gary, Bel, Ruby and Morris trudged home, superheroes no longer. Their dream hadn't even lasted a week.

TRICKLE TIMES TWO

On *Tumchester Tonight* the raid on the school was the top story and Dickie Trickle was interviewing Detective Rigley again. This time the policeman was wearing his smartest uniform, with a polished hat because his wife had told him to. He looked very important but he soon started sweating under the hot studio lights.

'This crimewave is getting worse,' said Dickie in a very serious voice.

'It is,' said Detective Rigley, dripping like a wet flannel. 'But we have made a huge breakthrough today. We have found a connection. That connection is . . . sweets.'

'Sweets?' asked Dickie.

'Yes,' said the policeman looking like a melted lolly. 'In the raid on Simpson's Sweet Shop, what did they take? Sweets. Only sweets. At the supermarket, did they steal money or jewellery? No. They just took . . .'

'Sweets?' said Dickie.

'Sweets,' nodded the policeman, drowning in sweat. 'And at the school today they only took sweets. So we are pretty sure the connection is sweets.'

'So what does it mean?' asked Dickie.

'No idea,' said Rigley. 'But I'm pretty sure they both like sweets.'

'Brilliant,' said Dickie in a way that sounded like he actually meant *I am talking to a man with a brain the size of a radish*. Then Dickie asked, 'We've heard reports of superheroes at the scene. Is this true?'

The policeman chuckled. 'You only get superheroes in comic books and movies, Dickie. Not in Tumchester.'

The anchorman nodded. 'So, what are you going to do next?'

'Find someone to turn the heating down,' said the policeman. 'It's like a sauna in here.'

Deep underground at Fluffy's Funfair, The Boss chuckled. 'Hlug, hlug, hlug, hlug. The cops are clueless and we are as cool as an Arctic fox eating frozen peas in an igloo with the door open and a stiff breeze blowing round his tail.'

His henchmen laughed.

'I learn so much from you Boss. I never even knew Arctic foxes ate frozen peas,' marvelled The Panteater.

The Boss was about to explain when something on the TV caught his eye. After interviewing the policeman, Dickie Trickle showed a grainy video taken at the school. In it you could see The Panteater and Jumper Jack Flash running to the Arts block and hundreds of children fleeing for their pants. Amongst the crowd, though, three small figures in purple tracksuits and masks seemed to be going the other way, as if they were chasing the crooks.

The Boss spoke to Jumper Jack and The Panteater very slowly. 'When you were raiding the school, you didn't come across any *superheroes* did you?'

'Can't say we did, Boss,' said The Panteater confidently. 'Nothing at all. Zero. Zilch.'

The Boss relaxed.

'Unless of course you count those little guys in masks who tried to stop us,' The Panteater continued. 'They *were* all wearing matching outfits. And one of them could fly. And another had a magic pocket. And the third one could swing about like a monkey. But apart from that there was absolutely nothing that I could see.'

The Boss jumped from his chair. '**NOTHING THAT YOU COULD SEE?!**' he shouted. 'Flying around in masks? Magic pockets? Leaping about like a monkey? **THAT'S EXACTLY WHAT SUPERHEROES DO, YOU IDIOT!**'

'Ah. Well. If you put it like that . . .' said The Panteater.

The Boss sat down, drumming his fingers on a heavy set of gold false teeth that he used as a paperweight. 'If superheroes are flying about, we need to speed things up, take things further, move to the next level. And fast!' His hideous, villainous laugh rang out. 'Hlug, hlug, hlug, hlug, hlug.'

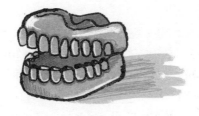

PARROT FASHION

The Boss needn't have got so worked up. Far from being ready to stop the crooks, Tumchester's only gang of superheroes weren't even on speaking terms.

At school the next day they did their best to ignore each other. At playtime Bel went to the school library, but whenever she tried to talk to somebody the librarian whispered 'Shhhhhhuuusssh.' Morris sat on a step and drew pictures, but it started to rain and they all got smudged. Ruby joined in a game of football with some boys and she scored a goal, but nobody patted her on the back and said, 'That was brilliant.' Gary hung about with Snoddy and Ferret.

'How come you aren't playing wimpy games with your wimpy friends?' asked Snoddy.

'No reason,' said Gary. 'They're just kids I know from Fish Street anyway. Thought I'd chill with you.'

Snoddy and Ferret said they should play something called Snakes Alive! and Gary's job was to keep a look out for teachers. The game was this: Snoddy would tell one of the younger kids that a deadly snake had escaped from the zoo. Then the child would be invited to sit on a bench, where Ferret was hiding underneath with a sprig of holly. As soon as Snoddy said, 'This snake's got fangs like screwdrivers and bites its victims on the bottom,' Ferret would jab the holly up and send the little kid squealing into the air. Snoddy and Ferret howled with laughter and even Gary thought it was funny at first, but when some children started crying he felt mean. So Gary pretended he had to go and find his jumper in lost property.

'No worries, dude,' said Snoddy. 'Catch you later.'

After school, the ex-superheroes all walked home alone. Normally they'd chat about the day's events with each other, but now there wasn't anybody to share their stories with. That night they were really down in the dumps. They'd all started to realise life without the other three wasn't much fun, but they were too stubborn to do anything about it.

It was a good job Cyril had more sense. He overheard Ruby tell her Gran that she wasn't friends with the others anymore and he quickly put two and two together. Usually when he did this, Cyril came up with 63, but this time he was spot on.

In the body of a parrot he couldn't do any magic, but he knew he had to do something. So, when everybody else in the house was asleep, Cyril sucked his feathers in and tried to squeeze through the bars of his cage. He wiggled and jiggled with no luck, but then he quiggled, miggled, shiggled and chiggled until at last, he plopped out like a bright green jelly from a mould.

Cyril took a pen in his beak and carefully wrote four letters: one from Ruby to Bel, another from Bel to Ruby, one from Gary to Morris and finally one from Morris to Gary. Each letter was the same, with only the name changed.

Dear Ruby/ Gary/ Morris/ Bel

You are my best friend and I feel really, really, really, really rubbish because we fell out. I would love it if we gave the Fabulous Four Fish Fingers one more go. And I know the others would too. We took a vow to help people in emergencies and I think we should really try to keep it. We are only beginners at being superheroes so we are bound to make mistakes. Meet me before school, in the field where we met that handsome elf Cyril. I'll tell the others.

Your best friend
Ruby/Gary/Morris/Bel

P.S Let's never talk about this letter. I'd be embarrassed if we did. It can be our secret.

Cyril figured that as long as they didn't compare the letters it should work out fine. It might have been a good idea if he'd also written something to tell the Fish Fingers about being trapped as a parrot, but he was too proud to admit he'd got into such a mess.

So, the only thing he had to do now was deliver the letters. Since it was midnight and he was locked in Ruby's living room that was easier said than done. But then he remembered how the real Marvin had got inside that creepy old house and it wasn't through the door . . .

JOLLY GOOD

When Ruby and her gran came down for breakfast, they found the parrot fast asleep and covered in soot.

'How can a parrot get that dirty inside a cage?' asked her gran. 'Looks like he's been up the chimney.'

'But that's impossible – the door's locked!' said Ruby.

'Nothing that parrot does surprises me,' said her gran. 'He probably belly danced his way between the bars.'

'Ruby, there's a letter for you,' Ruby's mum shouted from the hall. At three other houses on Fish Street, two other mums and one dad found letters just like it.

An hour later, Gary, Bel, Ruby and Morris sat under the tree that Cyril had once turned into a five-headed dog. Gary was first to speak.

'OK, I just want to say sorry for giving up on the Fish Fingers. You lot are like my family and I want us back together.'

The others smiled and Morris patted his friend on the back.

Bel said, 'Superheroes are supposed to be brave, but I was a scaredy cat. I really want to give the Fish Fingers another try and I promise to be tougher in future.'

'Even if there's a rabbit?' said Gary.

'**WHERE'S A RABBIT?**' screamed Bel, but the faces of her friends quickly told her there wasn't one.

Er . . . yes. I mean, YES! Even if there's a rabbit.

Everybody gave Bel a round of applause. Ruby spoke next. 'I never wanted us to split up in the first place. We are blooming brilliant together. We are! And we can help zillions of people if we try. We are the FOUR Fish Fingers and together we are FABULOUS!'

They clapped Ruby too.

Then Morris said, 'And I'm sorry for being . . . a bit of a Morris.'

Everybody laughed. The truth was, Morris wanted to be back in the Fish Fingers as much as anyone. Not because he wanted to be a superhero – he hadn't changed his mind on that – but he missed his friends.

Bel thought they needed some advice on how to be better superheroes. She said they should go and speak to someone clever who might be able to help.

'How about Mr Jolly? He's lovely and I'm sure he'll have loads of good ideas,' suggested Ruby.

The others liked Mr Jolly too, so they decided to talk to him at lunchtime. Of course, they couldn't let him know their superhero secret, but they hoped they'd be able to speak to him without mentioning it.

When they found Mr Jolly, he was sitting in his classroom marking spelling tests and counting out sweets. (He gave them to all the children who did well in his tests.) Mr Jolly seemed happy to help and the Fish Fingers gathered around his desk.

Bel began. 'We are in a team but we're not doing very well. We all have our own little problems and they keep getting in the way.'

'OK,' said Mr Jolly, thinking they must be in a football side or a Frisbee club or something like that. 'Let's try to fix your problems one by one.'

Morris said his trouble was transport. 'I can never get to where I need to be on time. I have to ask for lifts and it's not very reliable.'

Mr Jolly thought Morris must mean he was late for training sessions.

'That's easy,' he said. 'Get yourself a bike. I had one when I was your age and I pedalled it everywhere.'

Morris knew Slug Boy would find it tricky to pedal a bike since he didn't have any legs, but the teacher had given him an idea. 'Thanks!' he said.

'Who's next?' asked Mr Jolly, blowing his nose on a black hanky.

Ruby said, 'At the most important moments I get into a panic. I try to stay calm, but I can't. My fingers feel like sausages and I drop things.'

Mr Jolly thought Ruby must be the goalkeeper.

'The best way to deal with losing,' said Mr Jolly, 'is to carry on until you win. Of course, you also need to practise, practise, practise.'

Ruby nodded. Mr Jolly had given her a really good idea too.

Bel said, 'My problem is I'm scared of rabbits.'

Mr Jolly couldn't for the life of him see how this could stop anybody being good at football or Frisbee, but he gave Bel some advice anyway.

'Try to get used to the idea of rabbits a little at a time. Maybe carry a photo of a bunny around in your pocket and have a look at it every now and then.'

Bel promised to try.

'And what's troubling you, Gary?' asked Mr Jolly.

'He thinks girls aren't as good as boys,' answered Ruby.

Gary said, 'No! Well, sometimes.'

Mr Jolly said, 'It's true that boys are usually a

bit stronger than girls, but muscles don't make you tough. What counts is how much fight you have in your heart. Don't forget Tumchester is named after Tilly Tum, the girl who saved her sister from a giant octopus by banging it on the head with a saucepan.'

Gary thought about what had happened when The Panteater and Jumper Jack chased him down the stairs at the school. He'd blamed Nightingale and KangaRuby for tangling him up in the net, but he should have warned them he was coming through the door.

'You're right,' he said.

Mr Jolly smiled and said, 'I hope you win a few more matches. If you work as a team, I'm sure you will. And remember, don't bunch up, spread about, pass the ball. Or the Frisbee. Or the shuttlecock or whatever it is.'

Then he handed them each a chocolate mouse from his box. 'Don't tell anyone about my secret stash,' he said. 'I'd like to keep hold of my pants.'

TRAINING DAYS

After their chat with Mr Jolly, the Fish Fingers felt ready to get down to some hard training. They knew they had to go off and try to fix their own problems, but they also knew they needed to be better at teamwork. That was the only way to beat Jumper Jack Flash and The Panteater and it meant staying friends no matter what.

Morris spent the weekend in the garden shed, gluing, drilling and polishing. He fixed together a small box out of clear plastic, with a lid and a leather strap. 'I'll call it the Slugmobile,' Morris said proudly to himself. There were holes in the top so that Slug Boy could breathe and the strap meant that any of the Fish Fingers could carry him around on their wrist.

Bel spent her weekend practising how not to be scared of rabbits. She put a photo of a bunny by her bed and looked at it before she went to sleep even though it made her feel sick. She carried another photo around in her pocket and tried smiling at it every fifteen minutes, but even after a day, she still shuddered when she saw it.

Next Bel decided to go to a pet shop. The assistant picked up a very fluffy bunny with long ears and asked, 'Fancy a little stroke?'

Bel thought she'd prefer to barbecue her own leg, dip it in ketchup and dangle it in a crocodile-infested river, shouting, 'It's lunchtime, boys!' but she actually said, 'OK,' in a tiny voice. She didn't quite stroke the rabbit, she just patted it on the head with her finger. Still, it was a start.

At 36 Fish Street, Ruby was training too. First, she got one of her Gran's old handbags and tied it round her waist. There was plenty of stuff in it, from biros to bus timetables and six pairs of glasses, so it was perfect for what Ruby needed. Then she started dipping her fingers into the bag, taking something out, putting it back. It was boring work but little by little she got quicker and quicker. Soon Ruby was

98

like a cowboy ready for a gunfight. She stared at herself in the mirror. 'Are you talking to me?' she said, 'Reach for the sky!' She pulled out a hairbrush. Then a brolly. And a soggy tissue. Not quite the

weapons a gunslinger usually carried, but Ruby now felt set for anything. Or anybody.

Gary's training weekend was spent with his little sister Nancy, letting her choose ALL the games they played. To Gary it was worse than going to an army boot camp, because there he could have worn boots, not the sparkly princess shoes Nancy made him put on. He also had to wear a pink dress, silver tights and carry a wand. Later Gary had to take Nancy's dollies for a walk, sing them to sleep and change their nappies, while she stayed in the house doing DIY.

Much to his surprise, by Sunday Gary was having great fun, but Nancy had so many ideas it was impossible to keep up. One minute they were ballerinas, the next they were mermaids, then pirates, ponies and kittens. Then the mermaids threw a tea party for the pirates and Nancy made him Queen of the Mermaids, which meant he had to wear extra glittery eye-shadow and her new flowery swimsuit.

The doorbell rang and Gary left the Realm of the Little Fishes (Nancy's room) to answer it, still carrying a plastic teapot.

'O! M! G!' said Snoddy, who was on the doorstep holding a football.

'What's up?' said the Queen of the Mermaids. And then he remembered what he was wearing.

'I, er, thought you might be coming out,' said Snoddy. 'But I can see you're busy. What is it? Barbie and Ken getting married? Ballroom dancing practice? Or ballet at the bottom of the sea?'

Gary felt himself redden, but then he realised he wasn't embarrassed at all. In fact, he was starting to see things very clearly. 'Just hanging out with my sister,' he said. 'She's a girl and she's brilliant . . .

We're having a mermaid tea party.

'You'd better invite Doris round then,' said Snoddy. 'He's a big girl like you.'

'For the record,' said Gary. 'Morris is the best friend anyone could wish for. He's loyal, kind, brave and really, really cool. Because being cool isn't about socks or bling or hair gel. It's about what you're like inside.'

'Whatever,' said Snoddy. 'You get back to the mermaids. Their tea'll be getting cold.' Gary slammed the door in Snoddy's face and then collapsed in giggles. His training weekend had been time very well spent.

On Sunday night, The Fish Fingers got together for a meeting at Bel's house. First, everybody talked about the training they'd done and Morris showed off his Slugmobile.

'*Well* wicked,' said Gary, slipping it over his wrist to see what it felt like. 'Mozza, you're a genius.'

Morris beamed. It was great to be best friends with Gary again.

Then they all tried to think of a plan for catching The Panteater and Jumper Jack Flash.

'The trouble is they are always one step ahead,' said Gary.

Bel agreed. 'If only we could find out their next target and get to it first.'

'It could be anywhere that sells sweets,' said Morris. 'What are we going to do? Text them? *Hi*

*baddies, it's us, the goodies. Where RU robbing next?
Tell us so we can put U in jail. LOL. The FFFF.'*

The others laughed, but, mid-chuckle, Ruby
suddenly stopped. She'd had a brainwave. 'I've got
it!' she said. 'The next place they'll hit. It has to be!
It's bound to be!'

The others stared at her. If Ruby was right, it was
the cleverest thing she'd ever figured out and they'd
soon be face to face with the supervillains again.

STAKE OUT

Ruby was bouncing up and down with excitement. 'There's one place they haven't raided and it's got more sweets than anywhere in Tumchester. Sowerby's sweet factory!'

'Of course, *Sweet and Sowerby!*' said Bel. It was the firm's motto and printed on all their sweet wrappers. 'Well done Ruby. Really well done!'

'Nice one, Rubes,' said Gary. 'Girls do get brilliant ideas sometimes, don't they?' He winked and Ruby smiled.

They decided the best thing they could do was stake out the factory. So the next night, straight after tea, the Fish Fingers sat in a bus shelter, gazing at the magnificent building that had been supplying sweets to Tumchester for over a hundred years.

From the outside Sowerby's factory was like a fairy castle, with lots of little roofs, roses trailing over the walls and three tall chimneys puffing steam into the clouds. There was also a security guard in a blue uniform standing by a hut.

'What if The Panteater and Jumper Jack Flash wait until midnight before they come?' asked Ruby. 'I would if I were them. It's easier to skulk about. Villains love skulking about.'

'I don't think they care about that,' said Morris. 'They raided Fish Street School at eleven o'clock in the morning.'

The Fish Fingers waited. And waited. And . . . waited. Buses went past, the town hall clock chimed and the security guard paced, but there was no sign of any super villains (skulking about or not). So they all went home.

Later on *Tumchester Tonight* it said Jumper Jack and The Panteater had raided a bowling alley instead. The Fish Fingers came back the next night, but still nothing happened.

By the fifth night they'd spent so much time in the bus shelter that bus drivers ignored them and if they'd actually wanted to catch a bus it would have been impossible. The shadow of another bus drifted by and its tyres splashed through a puddle, spraying dirty water over the four friends.

'Hey!' shouted Morris and they all looked up to see that it *wasn't* a bus. It was an ice-cream van with

a big plastic cone on the roof and it was pulling up outside the factory gates.

'Is that them?' whispered Bel.

'It could be,' said Gary.

'J-J-J-Jumping jellybeans!' stuttered Ruby.

'I'm ch-ch-changing,' said Morris as his body began to wobble. Ruby's legs felt like rubber, Gary's hands started to tingle and Bel felt as though her body was floating.

On the other side of the road though, things were happening even faster.

The Panteater had parked and Jumper Jack had sneaked out of the back, slithering underneath the van. The security guard marched over, but soon wished he hadn't.

'Can I help y-**ERRRRRRR?**' he shouted, as Jumper Jack leapt from his hiding place and pulled him to the ground. Before the man could protest, The Panteater struck and gobbled up his pants. '*EEEUUUGGGHHHHH!*' he screamed.

'Let's go!' said Jumper Jack and the two villains clambered into the van and smashed through the factory gates, leaving the guard on the ground.

THE BATTLE OF SOWERBY'S SWEET FACTORY

KangaRuby bounced, Nightingale flew, with Slug Boy in the Slugmobile, and The Chimp swung over the road to the factory. First, they checked on the security guard.

'I th-th-think I'm fine,' he said. 'I just need a cup of tea.'

KangaRuby dipped her hand into her pocket and pulled out a jar of pickled onions.

'Will this do?' she asked.

'Ooh yes,' he said. 'I love pickled onions.'

The crooks hadn't wasted any time inside the factory. Three workers lay on the ground tied up in their green overalls. Another looked like he'd been stapled to the wall. He stood, arms stretched out, one trouser leg rolled up to his knee, mumbling, 'It grabbed my grundies.' Smashed crates, wrappers and boxes of sweets lay scattered across the factory floor.

In the middle of the room were three enormous machines: pink, green and blue. They were the heart of the factory and for over a century their belts had rolled, their clocks had ticked and their chimneys had pumped steam as they churned out marshmallows, peanut brittle, chocolate limes or any of the other yummy treats Sowerby's was famous for. But not now. The Panteater was clogging them up with tables, chairs, buckets, mops, brushes and broken boxes. Slowly the machines shuddered to a halt and began honking like lorries going backwards. Sparks fizzed from the machinery and leapt towards the ceiling.

Jumper Jack Flash was filling up the van. He'd already thrown in pear drops and pink shrimps, chocolate mice and chewy mints, and his hands were in a barrel of butterscotch when the Fish Fingers swung through the doorway.

'It's game over!' shouted The Chimp, as the villains turned to look. 'Don't move and put down your sweets.'

'I'll have to move then, won't I?' said the rabbit.

'Well, yes, a bit. But only to put down your sweets,' answered The Chimp.

'So, I can move?' asked Jumper Jack Flash.

'Yes, yes. Stop rabbiting – sorry, poor choice of words –' said The Chimp. '**STOP ARGUING!**'

'Step away from the machine, Panteater,' said KangaRuby. 'We're taking you to jail.'

'But I'm about to eat,' smirked The Panteater. 'Three pairs of pants on toast. Without the toast.'

Jumper Jack snarled, then cartwheeled across the floor. He landed on KangaRuby's shoulders and boxed her ears until they glowed. KangaRuby dropped to her knees as the villain tried to grab the sleeves of her tracksuit top but – just in time! – she flung him from her shoulders, right into the path of The Chimp who had swung over from a pipe that criss-crossed the factory. He kicked the rabbit **THUMP!** into a wall.

'Not such a funny bunny now,' laughed The Chimp.

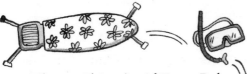

'Cheers, Chimp!' said KangaRuby, picking herself up.

'My pleasure,' he replied. It was fantastic when they worked as a team.

The groggy rabbit lay on the floor shaking his head as KangaRuby dipped into her pocket. She pulled out an ironing board. Once that would have slowed her down. Not now. Her fingers were a blur as she pulled out a spoon, a snorkel, a rubber duck and finally a skipping rope. 'This'll do nicely,' she said and tied the rabbit's hands and feet together.

On the other side of the factory, Nightingale swooped towards The Panteater.

'Try flying round him in circles,' shouted Slug Boy and Nightingale did just as he said. She flew inches above The Panteater's head, faster and faster, circle after circle. He kept turning left then right, right then left and got very dizzy.

I'll swat you like . . . er, a Fish! I'll sting you like a . . . um . . . giraFFe!

He was never quite quick enough to catch her. As The Panteater's head swirled, KangaRuby picked up a handful of gobstoppers and rolled them under his feet.

'**WHOOAAA!**' he yelped, slipping head first into a giant bucket of jelly-baby jelly. From the other side of the room, The Chimp hurled a bunch of coconuts and, as the gasping Panteater stood up from the gloop, one hit him between the eyes.

THONK!

The hairy henchman tumbled back into the jelly again.

'We're totally **FABULOUS!**' shouted The Chimp, punching the air like he'd scored in a cup final.

'We are the chuffin' champions!' yelled KangaRuby.

'It's all down to teamwork,' said Nightingale, patting KangaRuby on the back.

'I suppose we are pretty good,' said Slug Boy from the Slugmobile.

But it was much too soon to celebrate. Jumper Jack Flash had chewed through KangaRuby's skipping rope . . .

'Look out!' shouted Slug Boy as the evil rabbit launched himself from the rafters in the ceiling. He kicked out both legs, knocking The Chimp and KangaRuby flying towards the jelly-baby jelly, straight into the arms of a very angry Panteater.

Now Nightingale faced her rabbity foe. She started to tremble, but at that moment her training paid off. Nightingale looked the rabbit in his one eye and sang, '*DO-RE-MI-FA-SO-LA-TI-DO!*' so loud Jumper Jack felt like he was trapped in a fire alarm.

'*AAAAAGGHHH!*' he screamed and Nightingale knew she had the better of him. Unfortunately, her singing had also shattered the windows and now it was bringing down the roof. A beam caught Nightingale and knocked her sideways. She tried to stagger up too quickly; the strength left her body and she fainted.

Back in the bucket of jelly, The Panteater held KangaRuby and The Chimp in each hairy hand. His tongue found The Chimp's trouser leg and he shouted, 'Bottoms up!' before The Chimp's pants disappeared down his throat. The Chimp crawled over to the side of the bucket to recover.

'Two down,' yelled The Panteater.

KangaRuby squeezed her fingers into her magic pocket, pulling out a very slippery squid. When it saw The Panteater, the sea creature got the shock of its life, so it leapt onto the friendliest thing it could find – KangaRuby's face. The more she struggled, the tighter it gripped and KangaRuby bumped blindly into the side of the bucket before falling back into the jelly.

111

'Three down and all out!' shouted The Panteater, bounding over to help Jumper Jack cram more sweets into the van.

'We've got to GO **GO GO!**' yelled Jumper Jack. 'This place is gonna BLOW **BLOW BLOW!**'

The rabbit was right. The sparks that had been leaping from the top of the sweet machines had turned to flames.

'Looks like they're going to have a lovely bonfire,' said The Panteater. 'Shame we can't stay and toast a few pairs of pants on sticks.'

'Er, yes. It is,' said Jumper Jack, not wishing to offend his partner (although he'd rather have eaten his Grandma's verrucas). The crooks jumped into their ice-cream van and drove off, laughing about a job well done.

Luckily for Slug Boy, neither Jumper Jack Flash nor The Panteater had spotted the *fourth* Fish Finger. They'd both seen the Slugmobile hanging from Nightingale's wrist, but thought it was just a fancy watch. Now, Slug Boy gathered his strength and pushed hard against the lid. It flipped open and the little superhero wobbled out along the leather strap and on to Nightingale's fingers. She was still out for the count.

Slug Boy looked up and trembled at the size of the mountain he still had to climb. But he knew that if he didn't the Fabulous Four Fish Fingers would be cooked to a crisp.

Slug Boy now heaved himself, inched himself, wibbled himself up Nightingale's arm. He caught his breath at her elbow, then slithered on, moving slowly, slowly upwards. He stopped for a second time on her shoulder and looked around. He saw KangaRuby and The Chimp in the giant bucket of jelly. He saw the three enormous sweet machines, clanking and clattering, sending clouds of black smoke towards the sky, flames hungrily licking the shattered roof. Slug Boy pressed on. He crawled along Nightingale's shoulder, across her neck to her cheek and over to her lips. Exhausted, he poked his little sluggy head into her mouth and sat on her tongue. Then . . .

'*UUUUGGGGGHHHHHH!*' she spluttered, mouth twisting with the horrible taste, eyes opening wide. Slug Boy's plan had worked perfectly! Well, nearly perfectly. Nightingale spat him out and he shot across the factory, splatting on the huge, blue sweet machine.

'Ooh,' he groaned weakly. He wanted to rub his head but he didn't have any hands.

By now Nightingale was wide awake. She saw Slug Boy on the floor and rushed over to help.

'Very sorry,' she said, scooping him into the Slugmobile.

'S'all right. I'm getting used to it,' he replied shakily.

Next Nightingale heaved KangaRuby and The Chimp out of the jelly.

'I'll take Slug Boy and get after that van,' she said, leaving the safety of Sowerby's sweet factory in the hands of a pantless Chimp and a confused KangaRuby.

The wind whistled through the holes of the Slugmobile as Nightingale soared higher than the flag on top of the town hall. She spotted the van as it sped past Tumchester baths and she raced after it.

'We're gaining on them,' she cried. But just then a tingling, sinking sensation hit Nightingale's body. As her superpowers faded, she began to float gently to the ground.

Unfortunately, Slug Boy didn't. As he transformed, he shattered the Slugmobile and dropped through the sky like a grand piano. Arms flailing, hurtling fast, speeding up. No longer a superhero, not even a slug, but a schoolboy called Morris with very, very breakable bones.

Bel screamed, 'MOOOORRRIISSS!'

ROCKING AND ROLLING

'What was that?' asked Jumper Jack Flash.

'What was what?' answered The Panteater.

'I thought I heard something. A kind of **THUD** on the roof, then a whimper,' said Jumper Jack.

'Probably a pigeon,' said The Panteater. 'You worry too much. Here we are with a van full of sweets, factory about to blow, superheroes all beaten and you worry about pigeons. Just enjoy yourself.'

'Maybe you're right,' said the rabbit. 'I do need to relax.'

The ice-cream van sped up and Morris flapped about on the roof like a pair of trousers pegged to a washing line. Down below The Panteater smiled to himself and settled back. Just another ten minutes to the funfair. He noticed a split bag of chocolate-covered raisins on the dashboard and he slurped up a few with his long tongue. They were delicious, so he sent his tongue slithering out for more, but it was a twisty road and the sweets kept rolling away.

'Hey, look where you're going,' said Jumper

Jack Flash. The van swung dangerously across the road as The Panteater chased the little chocolates.

'Who's the one driving?' said The Panteater. 'I never tell *you* how to drive when it's your turn, do I?

Every time the van swerved, Morris rolled over the roof, fingers white with pain, trying to keep hold of the giant ice-cream cone. It was like doing the Hokey-Cokey at a hundred miles an hour, but if he lost his grip his dancing days would be over for good.

The chocolate raisins were almost gone, but The Panteater spotted a really big juicy one on the floor. His couldn't get it with his tongue, so he bent down to see where it was. At that moment, the road twisted sharply to the left.

'LOOK OUT!!!' shouted his friend. **'TREE!!!'** Jumper Jack Flash grabbed the steering wheel and the van skidded, toppling on to two tyres, just missing a huge pine tree. The Panteater jammed his foot on the brake and took a deep breath.

'That was lucky,' he whispered.

Jumper Jack wiped the sweat from his whiskers. 'Very,' he replied.

Morris wasn't quite so lucky. When the van skidded to a halt he lost his grip on the ice cream cone and was catapulted into the pine tree. As the van moved off he was still upside down, untangling his trousers from the branches. The villains were almost out of sight by the time Morris wriggled free and fell into the muddy field below, but in the distance he glimpsed them driving towards two huge iron gates.

Where is that? he thought. It was somewhere he'd visited when he was little, but he couldn't quite remember. He knew he had to see what was behind the gates, even though he had bruises everywhere and a grazed knee. Morris limped off up the road.

By the time he reached the gates the ice-cream van had long disappeared, but Morris realised where he was.

'Of course!' he said to himself. 'It's Fluffy's Funfair!' Fluffy's had closed down when he was five years old but he had happy memories of sitting in teacups on the merry-go-round. *The crooks have got to be in there somewhere*, he thought. *There's nowhere else to go on this road.*

Morris turned to go. It was a long walk home and very late, so he knew he'd be in trouble, but at least now he had some vital information. It could even make him a hero! He looked out over Tumchester and saw the twinkling lights of the houses and the flats in the distance. Then he saw a giant ball of fire leap into the sky and explode into a million silver drops. Clouds of smoke drifted upwards and the earth glowed red. Morris prayed his friends had escaped from Sowerby's in time.

HOME SWEET HOME

It was very, very, very late by the time Morris staggered into Fish Street and he could see the flashing blue lights of a police car parked outside his house. Nervously, he opened the door.

'I'm home,' he called.

The hall was suddenly full of people rushing from the living room to see him. There was his mum, his dad, Gary, Gary's dad, Bel, Bel's mum and dad, Ruby, Ruby's mum and even Ruby's gran.

'Thank the Lord, thank the Lord,' said his mum, kissing him so much she covered his whole face with lipstick. The she shouted, '**HOW** could you do this to me? **WHAT** were you thinking? **WHERE** have you been? **WHY** didn't you phone? **CAN 'T YOU SPEAK, BOY?**'

'Let me take it from here,' said a deep voice above the crowd. It was Detective Rigley, who'd been waiting for the fuss to die down.

'I need to ask you a few questions, Morris. But don't worry – your friends have been very helpful.'

Gary had told the policeman they'd all been

playing hide-and-seek near Sowerby's when Morris hid himself in an ice-cream van. They only found out that it was a getaway van for Jumper Jack Flash and The Panteater when it sped off.

The detective carried on. 'After the factory went up, we found your friends huddled together in a bus shelter. They were lucky. What we don't know is what happened to you and how you got back here.'

'Well,' said Morris, taking a big breath, 'I don't quite know myself. I was hiding in the van and then the doors closed and it started moving – soon it was going very fast. I was really scared so I kept quiet. After a long time it pulled up outside Fluffy's Funfair. When they got out to unlock the chains, I saw my chance and ran off. Then they drove inside.'

'Fluffy's Funfair eh?' said the policeman, making careful notes. 'And once they were inside where did they go?'

'I didn't see,' said Morris. 'I was too busy running away. I even hurt my knee.' He rolled his trouser leg up to show them his graze.

'You've given us an important lead,' said Detective Rigley. 'In fact, you've been a little hero and you should be very proud of yourself.'

Everybody in the room clapped and cheered. Gary's dad sang, 'For he's a jolly good fellow . . .' and the rest of them joined in. Morris shook so many hands he thought his arm was going to drop off.

'What happens now?' Morris's mum asked the policeman.

'Tomorrow morning I will lead a team of officers up to Fluffy's Funfair. We will arrest Jumper Jack Flash and The Panteater and I am sure you will see it all on *Tumchester Tonight*. Not *Tumchester Tonight* tonight of course. That was on tonight. *Tumchester Tonight* tomorrow night. In short, tomorrow's the night for *Tonight*, not tonight.' He started to pack up his pencil and his notebook.

'Can we come with you tomorrow?' asked Morris.

The policeman thought for a second. 'I can't see why not, Morris,' he said. 'It's Saturday so you won't be missing any school. And with fifty police officers on hand I don't think you'll get into too much trouble. I can even see it making a nice report in the police magazine. *Brave Rigley Shows Youngsters How It's Done*. Yes, you can come.'

'Thank you very much,' said Morris, smiling at his friends. They all grinned back. Morris closed his eyes and dreamed of the medal they would one day pin on his school blazer.

ALL THE FUN OF THE FAIR

At exactly 6:01 am, a crack team of fifty police officers arrived at the gates of Fluffy's Funfair. They came in vans, cars and minibuses. There was even a helicopter hovering overhead and a crane with a wrecking ball that swung from a long metal arm. Gary, Bel, Ruby and Morris sat in the back of a police van, watching what was happening through the window. They'd brought sandwiches, biscuits and cans of pop so it felt like a party.

Detective Rigley radioed the go ahead to the driver of the crane and it crashed through the rusty metal gates. The police officers moved like soldier ants across the fair. They searched every corner of every ride and then, to make sure they hadn't missed anything, they used spanners, hammers and the wrecking ball to break up the rides. They took apart the ghost train, the rollercoaster, the house of mirrors and the merry-go-round with teacups for seats. But after six hours nobody had found anything. They stopped for lunch and then they searched all over again. By five o'clock the police officers were very fed up. They shook their heads and kicked the floor. They hadn't found a single clue, not even a sweet wrapper. Of course, the one place the police hadn't searched was under the water in the boating lake . . .

The Boss, Jumper Jack Flash and The Panteater watched the show on secret cameras far below and they sniggered as the police looked in all the wrong places.

'What did I tell you?' said The Boss. 'They couldn't find a bag of chips in a chip shop if they all had chip detectors and there was a big sign on the wall saying *Here are the chips.*'

Jumper Jack Flash and The Panteater laughed.

'You are very funny boss,' said The Panteater. 'What's a chip detector by the way? Does it go bleep if it finds a chip?'

'I made it up, you fool!' said The Boss.

'Oh right,' said The Panteater, a bit disappointed. 'That's brilliant.'

The police van drove back to Fish Street and as it pulled up outside number 27, Morris didn't even have enough energy to wave goodbye to his friends. That night he buried his head in his pillow and his eyes made two big puddles of salty water. He thought he was going to be a hero but now he felt like a big, fat zero. Just like Snoddy always said he was.

UP IN ARMS

The rest of the weekend was very gloomy for the Fish Fingers. After being told off by Detective Rigley (and their mums and dads) for 'wasting police time' they weren't allowed out for the whole day on Sunday. They spent it staring out of their bedroom windows, watching rain trickle down the glass.

But by the time they walked to school on Monday they were in better spirits and their early morning chat quickly turned to The Panteater and Jumper Jack Flash. They all agreed that the setback at the fair wasn't going to stop them trying to solve the mystery.

'Ice-cream vans don't just disappear into nothing,' said Morris. 'So where did it go?'

'There must be a secret room at Fluffy's somewhere,' said Bel. 'We have to get back in to find it.'

'Well, we can't do anything this week,' said Gary. 'None of us are allowed out after school and it's the prom on Saturday. It'll have to be next Sunday.'

Even though the Fish Fingers had decided to forget about The Panteater and Jumper Jack for a while, it was impossible because everybody else was talking about them. The crooks were getting more daring by the day and at the end of the week there was a *Tumchester Tonight* special looking back at their terrible exploits.

'The crime wave has become a crime tsunami,' said anchorman Dickie Trickle seriously. 'In twenty three days The Panteater and Jumper Jack Flash have committed over 300 crimes. Every child in Tumchester has lost sweets or knows somebody who has. Sweet shop owners are running out of things to sell and at birthday parties kids now have cabbages and cucumbers wrapped up in pass the parcel. At first we grown-ups shrugged it off, saying "It's only sweets." We even had a celebrity chef on this programme telling us how to slice a carrot to make it look like a traffic cone and how to chop a cauliflower to resemble a tennis racket. But we were wrong. A carrot is a carrot and a cauliflower is a cauliflower, no matter how it's chopped. They'll never be as much fun as sweets.'

Dickie Trickle explained that sweet factories in other cities were now too frightened to send lorries to Tumchester and angry crowds were gathering at the town hall. He said a mob had marched to the police station and thrown things (mainly vegetables). A flying tomato had even hit Detective Rigley on the nose.

Detective Rigley was in the studio. 'There's no need for the flinging of salad,' he said. 'Policemen miss their sweets too, you know.'

Dickie Trickle asked, 'Have you any new leads?'

'Yes,' said the policeman. 'The tomato has been dusted for fingerprints, although it is a bit squished. My nose was also dusted, but the brush made me sneeze. Finally, my fingers were dusted for fingerprints – and we found some super ones – but they all turned out to be mine.'

'I meant new leads for the robberies,' said Dickie.

'Er, no,' answered the policeman. 'But we are sure we will crack this case sooner or later.'

'Before you go,' said Dickie. 'Have there been any more reports of superheroes? We heard there were three at Sowerby's sweet factory when it was raided. Can you confirm this?'

'I can confirm it is hogswallop, nonsense and bunkum.'

'Funny names for superheroes,' said Dickie.

'Er, I mean it isn't true,' said the policeman. 'There's no such thing.'

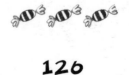

126

Deep underground at the funfair, The Boss was watching TV in the bath and chuckling to himself, 'Hlug, hlug, hlug, hlug, ooh the plug.' So he changed ends (he'd sat on the plug) and started laughing again. The Boss's henchmen had carried out his orders to the letter. Night after day, day after night, The Panteater and Jumper Jack had been out, stealing sweet after sweet after sweet. They'd brought back hundreds of bags to the lair, all unloaded by the robot mice, un-speaking, un-squeaking, never resting. Now the warehouses overflowed with all types of sweets from jelly babies to dolly mixtures, midget gems to wine gums, sugared almonds to lollipops and a mountain of sherbet so high you could go down it on a sledge. Soon there wouldn't be a sweet left in Tumchester and it would be time for the final, terrible piece of The Boss's plan. 'Hlug, hlug, hlug, hlug, hlug . . .'

PARTY TIME

Morris was in the bathroom getting ready for the prom. He was wearing his best (and only) jeans and he was trying to fasten the buttons on his shirt but they were putting up a fight. He had to suck in his stomach until his ears turned purple before he could squeeze the last one into its hole.

'Easy peasy,' he said to himself, then the top button shot off like a bullet, hit the mirror, bounced back into Morris's eye and disappeared down the plug hole. 'Stay calm,' he said to himself. 'It *is* the only cool shirt you've got. But you don't need that button. You're still loooooooking goooooood.'

He left the bathroom and walked straight into his dad, who was carrying an enormous ketchup sandwich. Morris's mum came out of the bedroom and saw what she thought was a bloodbath. **'CALL THE PARAMEDICS! SOMEBODY SAVE MY BOY! HIS LIVER'S BURST! HIS LEGS ARE EXPLODING! HIS STOMACH'S DROPPED OUT!'** she screamed, ripping off Morris's shirt and wrapping him in bandages.

Although peace returned to Morris's house when his mum learned the truth, he still needed to change his clothes. His mum tried to help by dressing him in one of his dad's shirts (sleeves rolled up) and some green velvet trousers Morris had worn to a wedding. His mum had made them out of a pair of curtains ('Nobody'll know,' she promised) and she finished off his outfit with some 'bling' – a chain that normally kept the garden gate shut.

Morris set off, prudently taking a bag with him that had a new Slugmobile inside (just in case of emergencies) and soon found Gary kicking a football in his garden.

Gary was in his new skinny jeans and he had so much gel in his hair it resembled a giant toothbrush, but even his dad said he looked brilliant. 'Loving the bling,' Gary said to Morris, pointing at the chain round his neck. 'But I'm not sure about those trousers. They look a bit like the curtains you used to have in your living room.'

'Do they?' said Morris. 'Can't really remember those. Anyway, er, let's go and get Bel.'

Bel was getting into a long sari the colour of bubble gum. It had gold, sparkly lace around the bottom which matched the stripes on her new trainers. Bel loved mixing up old and new, East and West, and she looked stunning. Morris rang her doorbell and Bel danced out.

'Come on, boys!' she said. 'Ruby's waiting.' Then she stopped and sniffed. 'Somebody smells nice,' she said. 'A bit like tomato ketchup. Is it a new deodorant?'

Morris blushed.

Ruby was wearing an orangey, greeny, purpley T-shirt she'd dyed herself and a pair of jeans decorated with silver stars – and, of course, her hat. She was wearing so many jangly bracelets she sounded like a herd of reindeer, but her gran said she looked like a film star.

'Which one?' asked Ruby. 'King Kong, Godzilla or Miss Piggy?'

Her gran laughed. 'You look smashing, that's all.'

The doorbell rang and Ruby kissed her gran.

'See-you-later-love-you-say-bye-to-Marvin-for-me,' she yelled, bounding down the stairs and out of the door.

As the Fish Fingers walked towards school, they were bursting with excitement. The prom was always the biggest and best party of the year and Mrs Pompidoor had promised this one would be unforgettable. They turned the last corner on Fish Street and gasped.

Wowzer!

Fairy lights hung from the school gates and twinkled like melting icicles. There was an enormous tent on the sports field, a bouncy castle in the playground and a steel band playing calypso music in the car park. The smell of beef burgers and sausages filled the air and a huge banner hung from the hall saying *Fish Street Forever*.

They ran up the path to explore. First they jumped on the bouncy castle and found it was full of soapy bubble bath. So they threw foam snow balls until they were exhausted and, giggling and soggy, then headed to the tent. There were dozens of stalls inside, including a beat the goalie, a pin the tail on The Panteater, a tombola and limbo dancing with a body-popping DJ.

Mrs Pompidoor made an announcement.

'Boys and girls, you may be wondering why the doors of the hall are not yet open. Well, I have a surprise for you – something that even the other teachers don't know about! I have been secretly stashing sweets in my office for the last few months and tonight we are going to share them all!'

There was a huge cheer. None of the children had eaten sweets for over a week. The headteacher carried on. 'So please everybody, follow me to the hall.'

As the Four Fish Fingers joined the crowd skipping excitedly towards the hall, they saw Mr Jolly walking the other way.

'Hello there,' he said. 'Isn't it exciting?'

'Super-duper-smashing!' said Ruby.

'Aren't you coming?' asked Bel.

'I'll join you in a few minutes,' said the teacher. 'I just need to phone my niece who lives in Australia. She's six today and I want to wish her happy birthday.'

'That's nice,' said Gary.

'See you all later,' said Mr Jolly and he wandered off to make his call.

GATECRASHERS

When the children walked into the hall nobody could believe what they saw. There were five long tables covered in the most fabulous, incredible, beautiful sweets. There were dark chocolates shaped like peacocks, dragons and butterflies, and white chocolates shaped like roses, angels and diamonds. There were orange sweets that tasted like blueberries and blue sweets that tasted like oranges. There were sweets that fizzed in your mouth and sweets that melted in your hand. From candy canes to cola cubes and butterscotch to bon-bons, it was a feast for the eyes, the tongue and the tummy.

The Fish Fingers eagerly lined up. They kept bouncing up and down as if they were on space hoppers and none of them could stop laughing (or drooling). But then Morris felt a sharp knuckle in his back. He turned to see Snoddy and Ferret, who'd shoved their way into the queue.

'Lovely outfit, Doris,' jeered Snoddy. 'Neat idea wearing curtains instead of trousers. But you need to pull yourself together! Heh heh heh.'

'Huh huh huh . . . trousers,' laughed Ferret, not getting the joke.

'Just get to the back of the queue,' said Gary. 'Or–'

'Or what, Queen of the Mermaids?' asked Ferret, giving Snoddy a wink.

'I'd rather be Queen of the Mermaids than King of the Creeps or Prince of the Picklebrains,' said Gary.

'What you talking about?' said Ferret menacingly.

The children were so busy squaring up to Snoddy and Ferret that they didn't notice two window cleaners arrive outside. They both had big moustaches, huge floppy hats and dark glasses – not the uniforms you'd expect. (Unless maybe they were Mexican window cleaners and these two were not. They couldn't have found Mexico on a map even if it was just a map of Mexico.) One of the window cleaners was big and hairy. The other had rabbity teeth. The bigger one leant back as if to throw soapy water at the window, but suddenly hurled his metal bucket through the glass instead.

KACHANGGG!

The pane shattered and fell like hailstones onto the floor. Then both window cleaners leapt into the hall and whipped off their disguises. It was The Panteater and Jumper Jack Flash! Children screamed or fainted or both.

134

Miss Diddle, the drama teacher, bravely jumped on to a chair and shouted, 'It's our prom night! And you are ruining it!' She tried to punch Jumper Jack on the nose but The Panteater saw her and wrapped his tongue around her feet, tripping her up and sending her crashing into a table of chocolate butterflies. Then he went back for her pants.

Everybody had their eyes on the villains, so nobody noticed The Four Fish Fingers dash behind the stage curtains. They could feel their bodies tingling with superhero power. The Chimp popped Slug Boy into the Slugmobile and Nightingale slipped it over her wrist. They were all about to race back into the room when Nightingale stopped.

'Wait! I've got an idea.'

'Make it fast,' said The Chimp, 'It's getting crazy in there.'

They could hear the children screeching and sobbing, tables being turned over and thrown against the walls.

Nightingale said, 'We have to let Jumper Jack Flash and The Panteater win.'

'What?' said The Chimp.

'You're joking, aren't you?' said KangaRuby.

'I'm deadly serious,' said Nightingale.

'You're deadly doo-lally,' said Slug Boy from the Slugmobile. 'We can take them this time!'

There were more yells from the hall and the sound of pants being slurped.

'*AAAAGGGHHHH!*' someone squealed. It was Ferret. 'He's got my undies in his cake hole.'

Just then The Panteater burst through the stage curtains, chased by Mrs Pompidoor who was whacking him with a broom.

'You dirty great big hairy bully,' she shouted, bashing him over the head.

'*OW OW OW*,' he squealed as Mrs Pompidoor hit him again. He fell to the floor and Mrs Pompidoor bent over to give him another good wallop, but he grabbed the end of the broom with his tongue and hurled her into the air. She crash landed in a basketball hoop and hung upside down, ten feet from the ground.

The Panteater turned to the Fish Fingers.

'You again!' He made a grab for them all but KangaRuby bounced, The Chimp ducked and Nightingale soared as The Panteater swiped at nothing.

'**G**RRRRRRRRRRRRR,' he growled, chasing after them.

In the hall it looked as if a giant had picked up the room and shaken it like a snow globe. Wrappers drifted in the air, sweets were scattered across every tiny bit of the floor. Dozens of children had been tied up by Jumper Jack Flash and they were rolling around moaning and groaning. Ferret was sitting under a table, muttering, 'W-w-wet and s-s-sslimy,' and Snoddy was trying to fan him with his jacket.

The Fabulous Four Fish Fingers stood in the middle of the room with Jumper Jack on one side and The Panteater on the other.

'I hope you like prison food,' said The Chimp, 'because you'll get it every day where you're going.'

'I don't mind it,' said The Panteater, thoughtfully. 'But Jack's a fussy eater. He doesn't even like cheese or cornflakes and as for . . .'

'Don't chat to them!' said Jumper Jack. 'Start clobbering them!'

He crouched into a karate pose and let out a hideous war cry, but at the same time KangaRuby dipped her hands into her pocket. With lightning speed she whipped out a bag of chips. No good. A vacuum cleaner. Better . . . A garden hose. Even *better!* She twisted the nozzle and squirted the rabbit full in the face with a blast of freezing cold water.

Yuuuuuuggghhhh!!!

'Hope you liked your *hare*-wash,' laughed The Chimp. 'But now you need a *hare*-dryer.' He picked up the vacuum cleaner and as the rabbit staggered forward, KangaRuby tossed the electric cable into his path. Jack stepped on the sharp prongs of the plug and screamed, '*AAAAAAGH!* **THAT'S MY LUCKY RABBIT'S FOOT!**'

'Not so lucky any more,' said KangaRuby.

Meanwhile, The Panteater was chasing after Nightingale, but as he closed in she suddenly took off and flew out of the window.

'Ooh! Flying home to Mummy?' yelled the villain. Then he turned to KangaRuby. They stared at each other from ten paces away. Everything went still. The Panteater shot out his tongue but KangaRuby was quicker. Her hand flashed into her pocket and pulled out . . . nothing at all. At least that's what she thought, until she found a tiny ant crawling over her fingers. The Panteater saw it too.

Get it away From me! I hate them. I'm allergic. It's giving me a headache already!

The Panteater's voice was suddenly drowned out by a cry for help.

'I can't hang on!' It was Mrs Pompidoor, still upside down in the basketball hoop. She was getting very tired and starting to slip.

'Er, don't move,' shouted The Chimp. He leapt at the wall, using it as a springboard to bounce on to the hoop. 'I'm going to hold your ankles and try to lower you down.'

Beneath the hoop, KangaRuby was fishing in her pocket for something useful. Her training was really paying off now because in less than three seconds she pulled out a parsnip, a banjo and a bike before finally dragging out an inflatable dinghy.

'Lovely!' she said and yanked the cord on the boat, filling it with air. Carefully, The Chimp lowered Mrs Pompidoor, then she leapt safely onto the dinghy.

'Oh, that was wonderful,' said the headteacher. 'Thank you so much.'

But the rescue had cost KangaRuby and The Chimp valuable time and the villains had escaped with their stolen sweets. The two superheroes raced outside, but there was no sign of the crooks – just black marks on the road where their getaway van had skidded. The two friends sat on the steps, heads in their hands. They'd been so close . . . But where were Nightingale and Slug Boy?

'I know Nightingale hates rabbits,' said KangaRuby, 'but I thought her training was helping.'

The Chimp frowned. 'Come on, we have to find them.'

'I'm already found,' said a voice from the roof of the hall. It was Nightingale's. She fluttered down, the empty Slugmobile dangling from her wrist, with its lid flapping open in the wind.

'Where's Slug Boy?' asked KangaRuby. 'Is he all right?'

There was a worried look on Nightingale's face. 'He's er . . .'

'Nightingale, what's happened to him?' demanded The Chimp.

'They've got him,' said Nightingale.

KangaRuby and The Chimp gasped.

BACK AT THE FAIR

Nightingale tried to explain. 'While you two were with Jumper Jack Flash, I told Slug Boy about my plan. You know, to let the crooks win. He thought it was a good idea so . . .'

'So where is he?' asked The Chimp.

'Inside the ice-cream van,' said Nightingale.

'Not again!' cried KangaRuby.

Nightingale carried on. 'We won't let the bad guys win really. I wanted them to *think* they'd won so we could smuggle Slug Boy back into the fair. I've hidden him in the glove box. That's the little drawer next to the steering wheel.'

'Oh no!' said KangaRuby.

'Oh yes,' said Nightingale. 'It's called a glove box even though people don't put gloves in it. Slug Boy told me.'

'I don't mean *Oh no! It's not a glove box* – I mean *Oh no! Slug Boy is in real danger!*' said KangaRuby. 'If he turns back into Morris while he's still in there he'll be crushed.'

'I hadn't thought of that,' said Nightingale, suddenly feeling awful.

'Sounds like he hadn't either,' said The Chimp.

'I said we'd meet him at the funfair as soon as we could,' she said. 'Once he's found the secret room he's going to open the door and let us in.'

'Right,' said The Chimp, 'we'd better get after him. We've got about fifteen minutes of superpower left.'

The ice-cream van was speeding through the lanes and, hidden in the glove box, Slug Boy was thinking through the plan. He was hoping that Jumper Jack Flash and The Panteater would drive into their secret room and then go and have a cup of tea or a bath or something. This would give Slug Boy time to slither out, turn back into Morris and open the door for his friends. The plan would work brilliantly so long as there *was* a secret room. And not just a really horrible hideout, like a dark, scary cave full of baddies with giant spider-heads who loved the taste of slugs. Slug Boy shuddered, but he tried to calm down.

'Sit back, don't panic, you'll be fine,' he told himself.

Unfortunately, at just that moment Jumper Jack Flash fancied a humbug. And he kept them in the glove box. He opened it, put his hand inside and touched something wet and slimy.

'*UGH!* That's **HORRIBLE!**' he yelled. He picked Slug Boy up (creatures with claws could do it easily), opened the window and hurled him outside.

'What was it?' asked The Panteater.

'A yucky slug,' said Jumper Jack.

'Oooh, they're worse than ants,' said The Panteater. 'Talk about something else.'

'All right I will,' said the rabbit. 'We're going on strike.'

'Are we?' said The Panteater. 'The Boss never said.'

'We are going on strike,' said Jumper Jack, 'because *I* say we are. I'm sick of us doing all the work while he sits around feeding his jellyfish.'

'But he's The Boss,' said The Panteater. 'He's plotting evil plans and planning evil plots isn't he? Somebody's got to do it.'

'Have they?' said Jumper Jack. 'We'll see about that.'

The villain wound his window back up and they drove on until they reached the old funfair. They passed the big rusty gates the police had smashed with their wrecking ball. They swerved round the rubble of the old rides and, as they reached the boating lake, the waters parted and they sped down

143

the tunnel. The van stopped at the bottom and The Panteater flicked a switch on the basement wall to slide the roof shut. Then they drove off to deliver their sweets to the robot mice waiting in the warehouse.

Sitting on the floor of the tunnel Slug Boy breathed a sigh of relief. When Jumper Jack had thrown him out of the window he'd been very, very lucky. It was a windy day and just before he'd landed, a gust of wind blew him backwards against the van door and he stuck there like a piece of chewing gum. When The Panteater flicked the switch to close the roof, Slug Boy slithered off as fast as he could slither. He now knew all about the boating lake and The Boss.

'I didn't think those two could have done it alone,' he said to himself. He wobbled into the shadows to wait for his friends. But at that moment a door opened somewhere and footsteps echoed off the walls. He stiffened. The footsteps were getting closer. If the crooks found him he'd probably be sprinkled with salt until he fizzed and shrivelled up. Slug Boy was too scared to move. He saw the legs of a figure dressed in black. Black shoes, black socks, black trousers. The shoes *nearly* trod on him, but they carried on past. Slug Boy wriggled against the wall.

Nightingale, KangaRuby and The Chimp were just around the corner from the funfair when their superpowers started to wear off. Nightingale floated to the ground, KangaRuby stopped bouncing and The Chimp swung down from a lamp post. By the time they walked past the rusty iron gates, they were just the usual variety of Fish Fingers.

'Right. How are we going to find the secret room?' asked Gary.

'I don't know,' said Bel. 'This is as far as my plan went.'

'I'm not even sure there is a secret room,' said Gary. 'If there is, why didn't the police find it?'

'Maybe because it's secret,' said Ruby.

'Or because there isn't one,' said Gary.

At that moment they heard the sound of rushing water. Gallons and gallons, slooshing around.

'Is it a tidal wave?' asked Ruby. 'We need to run for our lives! Find higher ground! Save the animals! **DOES ANYBODY HAVE AN ARK?**'

'Er, Tumchester's seventy miles from the sea,' said Gary. 'So you don't need to panic. I think it's coming from over there.' He pointed to the boating lake and the children gasped as they watched the water split in two and slide away underground.

'Jumping jellybeans!' cried Ruby. 'It's a miracle!'

Suddenly, from the darkness, a voice whispered.

'Is that you?' It was as if a fish had spoken from the depths of a black lagoon.

Is that you?

I asked first!

OK, it is us. Now, is that you?

OF course it's me! Get down here Fast. It's safe at the moment. But keep quiet — they could be back any second.

Gary, Bel and Ruby did just as Morris instructed and scurried down the slope. It smelt of drains, but soon they saw a light and Morris was standing under it. They gave him a very big hug when they saw him.

'Well done, Morris!' they all whispered.

'I'm so pleased you're all right,' said Bel, who still felt terrible about putting him in so much danger.

'Come on,' said Morris, 'we haven't got much time.'

They crept deeper and deeper into the tunnel, past dim lights that cast their shadows on the walls. Water dripped from the ceiling as they slowly made their way further into the hideout. There were doors everywhere and the Fish Fingers put their ears to them, checking for voices, but the only noises they heard were engines whirring and water flushing through pipes. They came to an enormous door with a sign that said Top Secret. Gary put his ear up to it. Silence.

'Let's have a look inside,' he whispered and pushed the door open very slowly. The room was even darker than the tunnel. Bel felt on the damp wall for the light switch. She flicked it and the Fish Fingers found themselves surrounded by teeth. Rows and rows of millions of gleaming teeth. Ruby screamed and the others grabbed her, trying to make her shush.

'Wh-who-whose do you think they are?' asked Ruby. 'And where are the mouths that go with them?'

'I don't know,' said Gary, bravely picking up a set. He held them up to the light and suddenly started laughing. 'They're not real! They're all false teeth!'

The others picked up a set each.

'He's right,' said Ruby. 'False teeth! My gran has got some and she puts them in a glass of water by her bed every night.'

'Why does she do that?' asked Gary.

'Maybe they're thirsty,' said Morris. They all giggled.

Ruby spotted a sparkly set behind a glass case, sitting on a velvet cushion with a little card.

To my only
Grandson,
Keep smiling,
Love Grandad

'I wonder whose grandad it is?' she asked.

'And why would Jumper Jack Flash and The Panteater need false teeth?' asked Bel. 'They've already got teeth. I've seen them. All sharp and pointy.'

'Maybe it's the other one,' said Morris.

'Which other one?' asked Bel.

Morris said, 'He's called The Boss and it sounds like he's the brains behind it all. He tells them where to go and what to do. I think I saw his legs just before you got here. All in black.'

'He could be The Panteater's grandad!' said Ruby. 'Or Jumper Jack Flash's.'

'Grandad or not, what we *don't* need is another supervillain,' said Gary. 'Or a super-duper villain to be precise. The sooner this is all over the better. Come on.'

He led them back through the door and into the tunnel again. They'd only gone a few yards when they heard villainous voices coming the other way. Gary yanked open the nearest door and the Fish Fingers all rushed through. Nervously, they waited for Jumper Jack Flash and The Panteater to pass, but they never did. Instead, they went into the room right next door. It was The Boss's office . . .

THE MAN WITH THE PLAN

Jumper Jack Flash and The Panteater found that The Boss wasn't actually in his office, so they sat down on his black sofa with the silver arms to wait. Jumper Jack flicked through a copy of the *Tumchester Evening Post*. It had the headline 'STILL WANTED' and their police mugshots were underneath.

'It's a good one of me,' Jumper Jack said. 'But not such a good one of you. You don't look evil at all. In fact, you seem to be smiling.'

The Panteater peered over at the paper. 'If someone's kind enough to take your photo, I think it's just good manners to give them a little smile,' he said.

'But you were sitting in a police cell and they'd just sentenced you to seventy-five years,' said Jumper Jack.

'I was only being polite,' said The Panteater.

'You're also waving,' said Jack.

'He waved at me,' said The Panteater.

149

Jumper Jack Flash shook his head and The Panteater wandered over to look at The Boss's raspberry jellyfish. He took a toffee apple out of his pocket and threw it into the tank. The jellyfish pounced and the water swirled and churned like a washing machine. Within seconds not even the stick remained. There was just the smell of raspberry. The Panteater stared into the water.

'Careful over there,' said The Boss as he walked through the door, but The Panteater wasn't expecting it and he jumped, knocking over a coat stand which toppled into the tank and the jellyfish swarmed and the water whirled and splashed again.

'Sorry, Boss,' said The Panteater, as the coats and hats floated on the waves then disappeared in the raspberry ripples.

'Forget about it,' said The Boss. 'Saves me feeding them tonight.'

The Panteater went to sit back down on the sofa and started picking his teeth with a pencil.

Next door, the Four Fish Fingers had discovered they were hiding in a cupboard full of brooms, mops and buckets. It was dark, but Gary found an air vent that he opened and light shone through it straight from The Boss's office. The Fish Fingers stood on tiptoes to see what was happening.

The Boss sat at his desk, picked up the big set of gold teeth he used as a paperweight and gave it a polish with his black hanky.

'Good work today,' he said. 'That'll teach them to throw a party and not invite Jumper Jack Flash and The Panteater.'

The rabbit stood up and cleared his throat. 'Boss,' he said. 'I've got something to say and you're not going to like it. Er, me and The Panteater are going on strike.'

'On strike?' said The Boss, the muscles in his neck starting to twitch.

'Y-yes,' said Jack nervously. 'We don't feel we're getting job satisfaction.'

'Satisfaction, eh?' said The Boss, his veins starting to bulge.

Jumper Jack Flash nodded. 'We're not happy in our workplace.'

'Well now,' said The Boss, his voice getting louder. 'Should I put a snooker table in your bedroom? Or bring round cakes at three o'clock or let you wear jeans on Fridays?'

His henchmen nodded. The Panteater said, 'Ooh, that all sounds . . .'

'**THIS ISN'T LIKE WORKING AT TUMCHESTER TOWN HALL YOU KNOW!**'screamed The Boss, slamming his paperweight down hard on the desk. It bit a huge chunk out of the wood. Next door the Fish Fingers grabbed each others' hands. The Panteater tried to hide behind his pencil.

Jumper Jack said, 'D-d-don't be angry, Boss. I'm loving the sweets thing, I really am. I've got sweets for breakfast, dinner and tea and The Panteater loves them too. He's not eating half as many pants and his tummy trouble is a lot better for it. But all we do is steal sweets and bring them here. I don't understand it. Do we sell them now?'

The Boss smiled. 'We don't sell them, Jack – we give them away for free.'

Jumper Jack looked like he'd been hit in the face with a cucumber packed in a snowball wrapped in a custard pie. Even The Panteater couldn't believe his hairy ears.

'**WHAT?!**' demanded the rabbit. 'We've robbed, nabbed and nicked, battled cops and superheroes, so you can give the sweets back? For free? Are you stark, raving . . .'

'Mad, Jack? Some say I'm madder than a mad March hare on a fact finding mission to Madagascar.'

'Yep,' said Jumper Jack Flash.

'But if you and The Panteater stick with me, we can take over the world,' said The Boss.

'Take over the whole world?' said Jumper Jack.

'Me, you and him?' He looked over at The Panteater who'd now got the pencil stuck sideways in his mouth and couldn't get it out. 'I don't think so.'

The Boss laughed. 'Don't worry. It won't be just me, you and him.' He took out a remote control from his pocket, pressed a button and a huge video screen dropped from the ceiling. 'We've also got these!' said The Boss. On the screen was the secret room full of false teeth.

'I see,' said Jumper Jack. 'Taking over the world will be a doddle now we've got loads of teeth.'

The teeth glistened in the shimmering light.

'You aren't just looking at a room full of teeth,' said The Boss. 'These are all the false teeth made in Tumchester over the last fifty years. Apart from the ones left in a few old heads.'

'Fantastic. Antique teeth. The only teeny tiny thing we need now is an army,' said the rabbit.

'You mean like **THIS?**' said The Boss. He pointed his remote control at the video screen again and it switched to the robot mice working in the warehouse. Suddenly, they all stood to attention.

'There are two hundred of them,' said The Boss. 'And they are not just programmed to unload sweets.' As he punched another button, the mice all opened their mouths to reveal razor sharp, metal teeth. They seemed to be grinning. 'These mice are my finest work and with their help, I promise, we **WILL** take over the world.'

'Lovely. Teeth and mice. But again, *how* exactly?' asked Jumper Jack.

The Boss sat back in his swivel chair. 'Every man, woman and child in town is now crying out for sweets. They are desperate. They sniff the air in the hope of catching the tiniest whiff of a caramel cup or a cherry drop.'

'Yew wight, Bosh, **kuk—kuk—k—RRRRRR!**' said The Panteater, who was now choking on the pencil in his mouth.

The Boss carried on. 'If we give them their sweets back all at once, they'll feast and feast for days. But the mice have coated every sweet with invisible, toxic powder that speeds up the way sugar rots teeth.'

'Ughugh,' said The Panteater who'd solved his pencil problem by eating it.

'Within hours,' said The Boss, 'everybody's teeth will fall out and they'll come running to us for false ones, on their knees.'

'Er, why do they want false teeth on their knees?' asked The Panteater. 'Is it so they can talk through letterboxes? Or eat biscuits off a coffee table without sitting down? Or . . .'

The Boss looked at his hairy henchman in dismay. 'For anybody who has missed anything, the

following evil plan diagram should make it clear.'
The video screen flickered again and up popped a
fancy graphic that said:

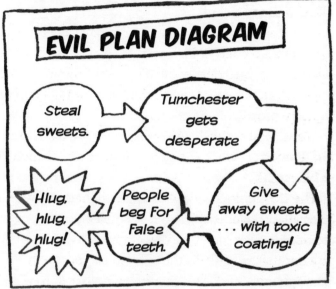

'The robot mice will make sure everybody pays
on time and we'll be rich, rich, rich! Hlug, hlug, hlug,
hlug,' chuckled The Boss.

At that moment something happened in the broom
cupboard that changed the lives of everybody in the
hideout. Sometimes the tiniest speck of dust can alter
the course of history and when it does people call
it the butterfly effect. In this case it was more a tiny
moth effect . . .

SEE HOW THEY RUN

In the Boss's office the villains suddenly heard someone say . . .

'**Achoo!**'

The Boss looked at Jumper Jack Flash. Jumper Jack Flash looked at The Panteater. The Panteater looked at the jellyfish. As one mind, they all looked at the air vent.

When The Four Fish Fingers had dashed into the broom cupboard they all thought they were alone. They were wrong. A tiny moth, no bigger than a fingernail, had followed them in. For a while it had flapped around silently in the dark, but when Gary opened the air vent, it was like a bottle of lemonade exploding in the moth's brain. Moths love light. They want to touch it, taste it, rub their noses in it, and this moth was no different. He hurled himself at the holes in the vent, but he kept bouncing off, flying in, bouncing off and, after his twenty-seventh failed attempt, the moth had a rest on Ruby's ear. Since this made it tickle, Ruby gave her ear a flick. The moth shot through the air at incredible speed, smashing into a shelf and sending up a cloud of dust. As the tiny flecks dropped like snowflakes, Morris felt a tingle in his nose telling him to sneeze. So he did.

It wasn't a very *very* loud sneeze. Just a little '**Achoo!**' and he might have got away with it. But in the darkness, Morris tried to wipe his nose, accidently poked himself in the eye, and fell backwards over a bucket.

As the crooks peered into the air vent, they saw three pairs of eyes staring back at them. They would have seen four but Morris was still on the floor.

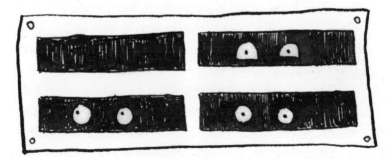

'Get them!' shouted The Boss and his two henchmen leapt into action.

The Fish Fingers started to get the shivery feeling that meant they were changing into superheroes again. The Chimp pulled open the door of the cupboard only to come face-to-rabbity-face with Jumper Jack Flash who wrestled him to the ground. The Boss grabbed KangaRuby and The Panteater wrapped his tongue around Nightingale.

'Drag them next door,' said The Boss.

Kicking and struggling, Nightingale, KangaRuby and The Chimp were hauled into the office and thrown onto the black sofa with the metal arms. The Boss picked up his remote control and quickly punched a button. A panel in each arm opened and two silver balls sprang up like Jack-in-a-boxes. The balls crackled and fizzed sending a laser beam between them and trapping the three Fish Fingers on the sofa.

The Boss stared menacingly into The Chimp's eyes. 'My advice is don't move, don't speak and breathe very, very slowly or you might find yourself fried alive,' he said.

The Fish Fingers all gulped. The Chimp couldn't move his body, but he could still talk and he was angry.

'We know what you're planning and you won't

get away with it,' he said.

KangaRuby joined in, 'You're all just nasty bullies and if your mums and dads knew what you were doing you'd be in very big trouble.'

'The police will stop you sooner or later,' added Nightingale.

'If the cops had more time they might,' said The Boss, sitting down and putting his feet on the desk. 'But time's up.'

The video screen showed the robot mice, starting to march, row by row, to the delivery trucks.

'The mice have tiny cameras in each eye so we won't miss any action,' said The Boss. 'I didn't expect an audience for my finest hour, but since you're here it makes it even better. There'll be no popcorn at the break, though, I'm afraid. Hlug, hlug, hlug.'

The Boss pressed another button on his remote and a huge map of Tumchester came out of the floor. There were tiny lights dotted along the roads and flashing red triangles at the end of each one.

'There are two hundred mice in two hundred trucks,' said The Boss. 'They will drive at top speed down these streets and park where you see the triangles. The people will smell the sweets and come out to feed like starving sharks at an underwater sausage sandwich factory.'

'It's going to be chaos,' said The Chimp.

'Exactly!' said The Boss. 'The more chaos, the more rotten teeth. The more rotten teeth, the more false teeth, the more false teeth the more demand . . .'

The Fish Fingers were too shocked to speak. The Boss was even more evil and despicable than they'd first thought.

'**Ugh!** What's *that?*' said Jumper Jack pointing at The Panteater's foot. 'I think you've stepped in doggy doo doo.'

The Panteater looked down and saw exactly what it was.

'It's another slug,' he said. 'They're everywhere today.' Slug Boy had been clinging to The Panteater's toe ever since the broom cupboard. The Panteater peeled the little superhero off his foot.

'Go and get some salt, Jack' he said. 'It makes them shrivel up, you know.'

'**NO!**' screamed the other three Fish Fingers.

'Oh, you like slugs, do you?' said Jumper Jack Flash with a sneer. 'You superheroes are all the same – a bunch of do-gooders out to save every creature on the planet. Well this sucker's had it.' He grabbed Slug Boy from The Panteater's claw.

'Leave him alone!' yelled The Chimp.

'Forget the salt, I've got a better idea,' sniggered the rotten rabbit. 'Time for a swimming lesson.' He dangled Slug Boy dangerously over the jellyfish tank.

'*STOP!*' cried Nightingale, but with a nasty smirk the villain flicked Slug Boy into the water.

The Fish Fingers screamed. The water churned and swished as the raspberry jellyfish pounced.

'What have you done?!' shouted The Chimp.

'He'll drown!' wailed Nightingale.

'It was only a slug,' said The Panteater. 'You need to worry about yourselves not some icky, sticky thing. That one was *really* ugly too. Funny eyes. Followed you round the room. Never seen one like that before.' He found a chair and settled down to watch the robot mice.

With tears in their eyes, KangaRuby, The Chimp and Nightingale looked desperately towards the water, hoping to catch the tiniest glimpse of Slug Boy. The water whirled and splashed, white foam bubbled on the surface and the killer jellyfish swished and swayed, but there was no sign of him. KangaRuby began to sob.

NEPTUNE RISING

Suddenly a little black shape shot out of the tank and landed on the carpet. The villains were busy watching the video screen so they didn't notice, but the other Fish Fingers did. Slug Boy lay on the floor, panting heavily. Then he looked up at his friends and smiled. They all started laughing. He must have tasted so horrid even the raspberry jellyfish spat him out.

'I'm glad you find something funny,' said The Boss. 'You won't be laughing soon. Not with your own teeth anyway. Maybe with a few false ones. Hlug, hlug, hlug, hlug, hlug.'

Slug Boy lay silently on the floor. He was still dizzy and there was water in his ears (well, the holes in the side of his head he assumed were ears) but he would be fine.

The video screen showed the last truck speeding through the gates of Fluffy's Funfair.

'That's the first part over,' said The Boss. 'It won't be long now.'

It was all very exciting for the crooks. The Boss

still had his feet up on the desk and he kicked off his black shoes. Jumper Jack Flash clapped his hands and The Panteater stood up from his chair to do a little dance. He wiggled his hips, then jumped in the air and tried to land on one leg, but he should have looked where he was going.

Slug Boy saw him leap and at that moment, threw himself under The Panteater's big, hairy, foot. It was an act of incredible bravery. The little superhero knew there was a chance he could be squished, but it was the only way to save his friends, Tumchester and the world. Slug Boy braced himself as the villain's foot landed squarely on his back.

WAAAAAAAAAAAAA!!!

The Panteater screamed as he skidded across the floor, crashed into the jellyfish tank and tumbled tongue-first into the murky water. It frothed like a stormy sea, waves crashed over the side, there was a yell and a terrible gurgling sound before suddenly it was calm.

The water cleared. The only things left in the tank were the terrible pink blobs and a few little hairs. Slug

Boy opened his eyes and sucked in a deep breath.

At first nobody said anything. One minute The Panteater was there and the next he was gone. Jumper Jack and The Boss walked over to the aquarium to take a closer look.

'It probably isn't how he would have wanted to go,' said Jumper Jack Flash.

'At least he didn't suffer,' said The Boss. 'Although he did scream a bit. And there was that terrible gurgling sound and all that thrashing about.'

'But accidents happen I suppose,' said Jumper Jack. 'Anyone can slip on a slug. Of course normally it would be in the garden.'

'Yes, I've never seen them down here before,' said The Boss. 'They are like buses. You wait ages for one, then you get three together.'

'There was only one,' shouted Slug Boy, sitting in the Slugmobile dangling from Nightingale's wrist. 'But I'm not the usual variety.'

The Boss turned to the settee where the silver balls now hung limply from two little wires. When The Panteater had fallen into the jellyfish tank he'd splashed water everywhere, soaking the sofa and blowing a fuse in the laser beam. The Fish Fingers were free and itching for a fight.

'You crooks might have all the false teeth in Tumchester, but this time you've bitten off more than you can chew,' said The Chimp.

'We're The Fabulous *Four* Fish Fingers,' said Slug Boy. 'And don't you forget it.'

'Four Fishy Fat Heads, you mean,' scoffed Jack Flash.

'The Four Floppy Fish Faces hlug hlug hlug' said the Boss, sniggering so much that his sunglasses wobbled. 'Jack, you get those two and I'll get the flying one and the slug.'

He leapt up to grab Nightingale's arm, but she dodged to her left and The Boss fell over onto the sofa, banging his head on a silver ball. Jumper Jack tried to trip up KangaRuby by crouching low and karate kicking her legs – but she saw it coming, bounced up, and whacked him with a rolling pin she'd pulled from her pocket. The Chimp swung down from the TV and grabbed the rabbit's fluffy tail.

'**GET OFF!** That hurts,' he yelled, but The Chimp tightened his grip. The badass bunny hopped around, shouting, screaming and swinging wildly, but he couldn't hit somebody who was behind him.

'Find something to tie him up, KangaRuby,' shouted The Chimp, as he danced desperately around the room with Jumper Jack leading the way. They tangoed, fox-trotted and cha-cha-cha'd while KangaRuby fished in her pocket and pulled out a light bulb, a jigsaw and a cornflake.

'No good. No good. No good,' she said, but she stayed calm and shoved her hand in her pocket one more time. She pulled out a cardigan with five arms. 'Perfect,' she said. 'It'll fit like a glove.'

Over at the sofa, The Boss was feeling better. He aimed his remote control at Nightingale who was flying overhead.

'Say "cheese",' he said and there was a blinding flash. Nightingale spiralled out of control, her eyes stinging, and she hit the floor with a bump.

'That's why I always wear sunglasses, hlug, hlug, hlug,' laughed The Boss. He pulled out a roll of sticky tape from his desk and sealed the Slugmobile shut. Then he started wrapping more tape round and round the groggy Nightingale.

The Chimp still had Jumper Jack Flash by his tail, but it felt like his fingers were about to snap and he suddenly let go. The crook wasn't expecting it and he ran headfirst into the TV screen, bouncing backwards into KangaRuby's arms. She rammed the five-sleeved cardigan down over his head, shoved his knees up and tied it round his waist.

'See how you like it,' she said, but Jumper Jack was out cold.

'Over here,' shouted Slug Boy. '**HELP!**'

KangaRuby and The Chimp turned to see The Boss had almost finished wrapping Nightingale up with sticky tape.

'Nearly ready for posting,' laughed The Boss, 'but what she needs is a stamp!' And he raised his foot in the air.

The Chimp dived at The Boss and the two of them grappled like wrestlers, but The Chimp was more nimble and he pinned The Boss to the floor. KangaRuby found The Boss's sticky tape and wrapped it around him.

'Now it's *your* turn,' she said.

The Chimp found a pair of scissors in The Boss's desk and cut Nightingale free while KangaRuby let Slug Boy out and put him on the desk. On the video screen, the trucks were still speeding towards Tumchester and on The Boss's map the tiny lights were getting much closer to the flashing triangles.

'They can't be far away,' said The Chimp.

'What are we going to do?' asked Nightingale. 'There are two hundred emergencies happening at once and we'll never get to them all in time.'

The Boss cackled. 'Whatever you do, it'll be too late.'

'Maybe not,' said The Chimp. 'Hand over your remote control.'

'Never,' said The Boss. KangaRuby bounced over and searched his pockets. It made a nice change from searching her own pockets.

'You're tickling,' said The Boss, just as KangaRuby found the device in his jacket.

'There has to be a button on here somewhere that will stop them,' she said. 'We just have to find it.'

'What about that big red one with "STOP" written on it?' asked Nightingale.

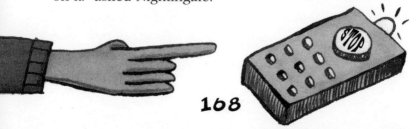

'Yes, possibly that one,' said Slug Boy. The Chimp jabbed it with his finger and instantly it turned off the TV.

'Just a bit too easy I guess,' said KangaRuby.

The Boss cackled again. 'You'll never figure it out,' he shouted. 'You don't have the wisdom!'

The superheroes decided to hit every button there was and then hit them all again. The lights went on and off, the TV shot through the ceiling, then popped up again, The Boss's chair burst into flames and a little windscreen wiper dropped down onto the jellyfish tank and started cleaning it. No matter which buttons they pushed, the lights on the map kept blinking, the red triangles carried on flashing and the robot mice drove faster and faster into Tumchester.

'We'll never work it out,' sighed Slug Boy.

The Chimp started to talk as he turned to face The Boss. 'It's over now so . . .'

But The Chimp was talking to a man who wasn't there. The Boss had vanished and the sticky tape was lying shredded next to the scissors.

'Jumping jellybeans,' cried KangaRuby. 'We've had it.'

ONCE BITTEN

Nightingale suddenly had an idea. 'Maybe it's not *this* remote control – maybe there's another one somewhere,' she said.

'That makes sense,' said KangaRuby. 'We've got two at home. One for the TV and one for the DVD player.'

The Fish Fingers checked under the jellyfish tank and down the back of the sofa. They pulled open the desk drawers and rummaged around in the filing cabinets.

'This is hopeless,' said Slug Boy. 'And we're running out of time!'

On the map, the little lights were almost touching the red triangles. Tumchester was about to be plunged into chaos.

KangaRuby picked up the grinning set of gold false teeth The Boss used as a paperweight.

'He's laughing at us somewhere. What did he say? You'll never work it out because you don't have the wisdom.'

'That's it!' said Nightingale. 'Maybe he was teasing us? Maybe wisdom is the answer.' She looked at the paperweight. 'Or, at least, wisdom *teeth*! Does that thing open?'

KangaRuby put the gold false teeth on the desk and with a little push, they clicked apart like an oyster shell.

'What are wisdom teeth again?' asked The Chimp.

'My dad's had his out,' said Slug Boy.

'There are four,' said Nightingale. 'You get them right at the back of your mouth when you're old. Top and bottom, left and right. Try pushing them, like buttons on a remote.'

The Chimp put his finger on a wisdom tooth and it moved easily. The trucks on the TV screen all swerved left.

'Nearly!' shouted Nightingale. 'There must be one to stop them.'

The Chimp pushed a second wisdom tooth and the trucks all swerved to the right. He jabbed another and their headlights came on.

'Only one left. Here goes!' said The Chimp. He took a deep breath and punched the last tooth. Instantly, the mice all beeped their horns.

'What now?' yelled Slug Boy. 'It didn't work!'

The Fish Fingers looked desperately at the TV screen. The trucks had arrived. The little lights on

The Boss's map had gone as far as the flashing red triangles and the robot mice all got out. They kept saying, 'You have reached your destination. You have reached your destination.'

In seconds Tumchester would be a disaster zone.

'Try pressing them all at the same time!' shouted KangaRuby. 'Quick! All four together!'

The Chimp tried to do as KangaRuby said, but in the panic he dropped the teeth and they rolled under the desk.

'*AAAGH!*' he yelled.

The mice were marching towards the doors at the back of the trucks.

The Chimp hit the floor and found the teeth, 'Which four was it again?'

'The ones at the back!' answered the others.

Some of the mice had their hands on the truck doors, as The Chimp jabbed his trembling fingers on the teeth. The Fish Fingers closed their eyes and held their breath. Immediately, the mice stopped. They stopped walking, stopped talking and they even stopped looking quite so creepy. If The Chimp had hesitated a moment longer, The Boss's evil plan would have worked.

The superheroes celebrated.

'**WE DID IT!**' they shouted. They laughed, giggled, jumped up and down, high fived and danced a conga around the office, dodging the groaning rabbit-filled, five-armed-cardigan shape rolling about on the floor. They even kissed Slug Boy on the cheek, ignoring how disgusting he tasted.

'Well done, KangRuby,' said The Chimp. 'What gave you the idea of pressing all four teeth together?'

'It was just a guess,' she said. 'But as teamwork is the best thing for superheroes, I figured it might be the same for teeth.'

ALL'S WELL THAT NEARLY ENDS WELL

That night the Fish Fingers gathered at Bel's house to watch a special edition of *Tumchester Tonight*. Once again, Detective Rigley was being interviewed by Dickie Trickle.

'You must be very pleased to finally get your rabbit,' said Trickle.

'We are,' said Rigley. 'He's behind bars now and that's where he'll stay.'

'What gave you the breakthrough?'

'It was brilliant police work, tremendous detective skills, incredible investigating and, er, a tiny tip off.'

'A tip off?' said Dickie.

'Yes,' said Rigley. 'We got a mysterious phone call telling us we'd find Jumper Jack Flash tied up in a cardigan, under the boating lake at Fluffy's Funfair. Our caller also told us about a map that would lead us to the stolen sweets. We very cleverly worked out the rest by ourselves.'

'Quite a big tip off, then,' said Dickie. 'But what about The Panteater?'

'I can't go into details,' said the policeman. 'However, the people of Tumchester can now sleep soundly in their pants.'

'So, is it case closed?' asked Trickle.

'I'm afraid not,' said Rigley. 'Our caller told us about an evil mastermind, who plotted the whole operation. He is known only as The Boss and, I'm sorry to say, he escaped.'

At Bel's house, Gary slurped the last of some fizzy orange that Bel's mum had made them.

'It's been a great day,' he said, 'but I'd love to know what happened to The Boss.'

'He could be anywhere,' said Ruby. 'Like Africa or a desert island or outer space.'

'I don't think we'll ever know,' said Morris, who was chasing the ice at the bottom of his glass with a straw. 'And we'll never be completely safe while he's out there.'

Bel's eyes suddenly sparkled with an idea. 'There's somebody who might help us find him!' she said, 'and it's not Detective Rigley or even Jumper Jack Flash.'

'Who then?' asked Gary.

'Cyril,' said Bel. 'Elves know a lot of stuff.'

'But we don't know where Cyril is either,' said Morris.

'My gran always says if you've lost something you

should look in the last place you had it,' said Ruby. 'And the last place we had Cyril was that creepy old house in the fields.'

'Maybe he's left Mr Snuggles inside the record player again,' said Bel. 'He is very forgetful.'

'It's a long shot,' said Gary. 'But, it's the only shot we've got. Let's nip over there first thing tomorrow.'

GRILLED
FISH FINGERS

Bright and early the next day Gary, Bel, Ruby and
Morris made their way through the fields to the old
house. Ruby was pushing Marvin in the pram because
she thought he could do with some fresh air. The
last time she'd taken him for a walk was over three
weeks ago – and a lot had happened since then. They
sneaked through the broken planks in the fence again
and Gary pushed open the front door. Then the four
friends and one caged parrot stepped inside.

Their shoes left footprints in the dust as they
picked their way across the rubble and kicked the
little white stones that looked like teeth. Slowly their
eyes got used to the gloom and they wandered into
the living room.

'What was that?' asked Ruby.

'What was what?' asked Gary.

'I thought I heard footsteps,' said Ruby.

'Probably ours,' said Morris. 'These floorboards
are very creaky.'

'MAAAARVIN'S STAAAARVIN, MAAARVIN'S

STAAAAAAARVIN!' squawked the parrot.

The old record player was still in the corner and the four friends headed towards it.

'Mr Snuggles was inside here last time, so if we're lucky . . .' said Gary. He pushed his fingers into the brass horn, but he soon brought them out, clutching nothing. 'It was worth a try,' he said.

'There it is again,' said Ruby. 'I'm sure I heard something creak. Coming from upstairs.'

'I'll bet it's Cyril!' said Bel.

They all stood and listened. Ruby was right. They could all hear it now. It was definitely the sound of footsteps on floorboards and it was getting louder.

'MAAAARVIN'S STAAAARVIN, MAAAARVIN'S STAAAARVIN, MARVIN'S STARVIN!' shrieked the parrot again.

'Shush,' said Ruby, putting his cage on the floor.

The Fish Fingers felt their bodies tingle. Morris wobbled and shrank, Bel found herself two feet off the ground, Ruby started bouncing and Gary began scratching under his armpit. The creaking footsteps got louder and louder. Marvin squawked and whistled and flapped his wings and – transformation now complete – The Chimp popped Slug Boy into the Slugmobile. The footsteps were outside the living room now and the Fish Fingers all held their breath. The door squeaked open and in walked . . . Mr Jolly.

'Mr Jolly!' shouted The Chimp.

'Dancing dandelions!' said KangaRuby. 'We were a bit scared.'

'Sorry, but do I know you?' asked Mr Jolly.

The Fish Fingers remembered they were wearing their masks, so of course Mr Jolly wouldn't know who they were.

'We saw you at the school prom,' said The Chimp. 'We were fighting The Panteater and Jumper Jack Flash.'

'Ah yes of course,' said Mr Jolly.

'We didn't expect to find you here,' said KangaRuby.

'Nor I you,' said the teacher.

'We were hoping to meet somebody who could lead us to The Boss,' said Nightingale.

'He's the evil mastermind who escaped. But don't worry, we'll find him one day.'

'I think we already have,' said Slug Boy. 'Don't you, Mr Jolly?'

The other Fish Fingers didn't quite understand what Slug Boy was saying, but it sounded a bit rude and Mr Jolly seemed very confused. He didn't say anything. He just stared at Slug Boy.

Well, Jolly?

'Steady on,' said KangaRuby. 'That's not so friendly.'

'I don't really mind,' said Mr Jolly. 'Because he's absolutely right.' He tugged at his wispy vanilla hair and peeled it off. It was a wig! Underneath he was all ginger. Then he took off his beige shirt and jacket and turned them inside out. They were black. He did the same with his socks and his shoes and even his trousers (they could see he was wearing black underpants). KangaRuby, Nightingale and The Chimp couldn't believe what they were seeing. Then Mr Jolly put on his dark sunglasses.

'Maybe you recognise me **NOW!**' said The Boss.

'I don't understand,' said The Chimp.

'I do,' said Slug Boy. 'It all makes sense. There were plenty of clues – we just didn't put them together in time.'

'What clues, Slug Face?' snarled The Boss.

'On the day Jumper Jack Flash and The Panteater raided Fish Street School, Mr Jolly took his cat to the vets *or so we were told,*' said Slug Boy. 'But I don't think he's got a cat because he's never got cat hairs on his jumpers. People with cats always do.'

'I do,' said Nightingale.

'He was unlocking the school gates for his horrible henchmen,' said Slug Boy. 'That's why they weren't smashed.'

'Excellent,' said The Boss. 'Any more?'

'Plenty,' said Slug Boy. 'Mr Jolly always wears beige. But I saw him blowing his nose with a black hanky.'

'Very clever, Captain Wobblebottom, or whoever you are,' said The Boss. 'My other hanky must have been in the wash. Now, is that it?'

'There was one last clue,' said Slug Boy. 'The sweets at the prom were a secret, so somebody must have told Jumper Jack Flash and The Panteater about them. Mr Jolly disappeared to phone his niece in Australia, but it was five o'clock in the evening and that's three o'clock in the morning over there. His niece must be a one-eyed rabbit or an anteater who eats pants.'

The Boss clapped his hands. 'Bravo. You'd make a first class detective. Shame you won't live long enough to join the police.'

The Boss took out a silver remote control from his pocket. 'I use this one for emergencies,' he said, pressing a button.

Three robot mice with glowing red eyes emerged from a secret panel in the wall. They were even bigger and more evil-looking than the ones who'd been driving the delivery trucks.

Marvin squawked and shrieked and rang his little bell, but nobody paid him any attention. There were more important things to think about.

'These mice have laser beams in their eye sockets that can cut through an oak tree,' said The Boss. 'Please don't move, or they *will* stop you.'

The Fish Fingers froze.

'Now I've listened to your claptrap about clues, so let me tell you a story,' said The Boss as he picked up a handful of the little white stones from the floor. 'Do you see these?' he said, waving them under their noses.

The Fish Fingers looked closely and saw that they were actually teeth. False teeth.

'This place is where my grandfather lived and worked all his life,' said The Boss. 'He was the finest false tooth maker in Tumchester. To him, teeth were like precious jewels, and he would shape, file and polish them until they sparkled. Everybody knew him, everybody loved him, everybody *needed* him.'

None of the Fish Fingers dared to speak in case they triggered the laser beams.

The Boss carried on. 'But then the world turned its back on him. People were cleaning their teeth twice a day, gargling, using electric toothbrushes. Suddenly their teeth weren't rotting and they didn't need false teeth any more. My grandfather died a sad and lonely man. On his deathbed I vowed to take revenge. I promised to take over the world with false teeth and I was very close to doing just that, until you lot came along.'

The Fish Fingers felt very sorry for The Boss's grandad but they still didn't think it made it OK to take over the world. Or even Tumchester.

'What are you going to do with us?' asked The Chimp.

'I've got a very fiendish plan for you all,' said The Boss. 'But first I am going to teach Mr Sluglock Holmes a lesson. Since I used to be a teacher, I think I'm the perfect person to do it.'

He got a pair of tweezers from his jacket pocket and plucked Slug Boy out of the Slugmobile. The Chimp raised his hand to stop him, but a robot mouse blinked his eyes and zapped his fingers with a red laser beam.

'*OW!*' he yelped.

'The mice are only programmed to stun at the moment,' said The Boss, 'but any more monkey business and you'll have toasted toes for tea. Do you understand?' They nodded. Then The Boss carried Slug Boy over to the old record player.

'You're just a rotten, horrible loser,' yelled The Chimp.

'And a big bully!' shouted Nightingale.

'So pick on someone your own size,' added KangaRuby.

'I think I'd rather pick on someone sausage size!' laughed The Boss.

'MAAARVIN'S STAAARVIN, MAAARVIN'S STAAARVIN!' squawked Marvin, hopping about in his cage.

'Quiet! The lot of you!' yelled The Boss. 'I want to listen to some music.' He quickly sellotaped Slug Boy to a record and placed it on the record player. Then he wound the handle and the turntable started to spin. Slug Boy's head swirled. Finally The Boss picked up the metal arm with the needle on the end and lowered it onto the record.

The Fish Fingers squeezed their eyes shut. They knew that as the music played, the sharp needle

184

would move slowly across the record and when it came to Slug Boy it wouldn't stop.

TIDDLY POM TIDDLY POM TIDDLY POM POM POM...

It was the same tune the Fish Fingers had heard three weeks before. Back then they were full of joy, now tears rolled down their cheeks. The record turned, the music played and Slug Boy got dizzier and dizzier.

TIDDLY POM TIDDLY POM TIDDLY POM POM POM...

Slug Boy tried to wriggle away but his head was spinning so much he didn't know where to go.

TIDDLY POM TIDDLY POM TIDDLY POM POM POM...

The needle was getting closer and closer and the little superhero trembled.

The Boss smiled thinly.

'It's time to say goodnight and good riddance,' he said, as the needle came within a whisker of Slug Boy.

'**STOP IT!**' shouted KangaRuby.

But the Boss just laughed, 'Hlug, hlug, hlug, hlug.'

TIDDLY POM TIDDLY POM TIDDLY POM POM POM...

Slug Boy knew the next time the needle came round would be the last. He closed his eyes.

FLASH BANG WALLOP

There was a flash, a loud **BANG** and a cloud of white smoke. It was Cyril!

'Hello there,' he said, stopping the record player with a click of his fingers. The needle lurched to a halt just brushing Slug Boy's little nose. The Boss pointed his remote control at Cyril, but the elf hurled his dust and the device shattered in The Boss's hand, the pieces turning into silver butterflies that fluttered out of the room.

The Fish Fingers cheered and Cyril pirouetted like a ballerina and let fly with more elf dust at the robot mice. As the glittering specks hit their targets the mice became tiny ladybirds and they scattered through the floorboards. Lastly Cyril turned to The Boss, who'd decided it was about time to run away.

'Not so fast!' said Cyril. Green lightning bolts flew from his fingers and struck The Boss, who turned into a giant snowman. He had buttons for eyes, a carrot for a nose and a banana for a mouth.

It's F-F-F-Freezing – and I F-F-Feel very s-s-s-silly.

Cyril picked Slug Boy up off the record player and sat him on the sofa, as the other Fish Fingers gathered round.

'Thanks very much, Cyril,' said Slug Boy, who was still a bit giddy. 'I was very pleased to see you and I never thought I'd be saying *that!*'

'You were brilliant,' said The Chimp, patting Cyril on the back.

'Our hero,' said KangaRuby.

'But how did you know we needed help?' asked Nightingale.

'I'll let you into a secret,' said Cyril. 'I've been in Tumchester all along. I swapped places with Marvin just to keep an eye on you. He's back now, though.'

KangaRuby picked up the parrot's cage where the real Marvin was now happily ringing his little bell.

'The trouble was, I forgot how to swap back,' said Cyril. 'The un-parrot spell is one you have to do in your head. Basically, you have to divide three zebras by two strawberry yoghurts then add x to y, where x is a traffic warden and y is a lawn mower. Easy if someone tells you, right?'

They looked at him blankly.

'So anyway,' said Cyril, 'it's a good job I heard the music from the elf record player. It's an antique,

187

made long before I was born and the music has very special powers. To an elf, hearing it is like drinking powerful medicine. Just the boost my memory needed.'

'But why is an elf record player here?' asked Nightingale.

'Because I gave it to The Boss's grandad fifty years ago,' said Cyril.

'**WHAT?!**' said the Four Fish Fingers together.

'W-w-w-what?!' shivered the snowman Boss and Cyril turned to look at him. 'It was the least I could do after your grandad made me these beautiful false teeth,' he said, smiling at everybody.

'You've got false teeth?' asked The Chimp.

'Too many sweets when I was a young elf,' said Cyril. 'They rotted away.' Cyril took his false teeth out to show the Fish Fingers.

Then the elf turned to the snowman Boss again. 'Your grandad was a good man, but you were right when you said he died feeling sad and lonely. It wasn't because the world had turned its back on him, though. It was because his only grandson kept being naughty and he was worried the boy would grow up to be a nasty old crook.'

'L-l-l-liar,' said the snowman Boss, but in his heart he knew the elf was telling the truth because elves don't tell fibs. Not big ones anyway.

'Come on, kids' said Cyril. 'Let's go and find a shady spot to watch the police cars arrive.'

It wasn't long before Cyril, Gary, Bel, Ruby and Morris were sitting under an oak tree watching Detective Rigley bring The Boss out of the house in handcuffs. The Boss wasn't a snowman anymore but he was still soggy and his shoes squelched as he walked.

'Now, how are we going to celebrate?' asked Cyril.

'Well,' said Gary. 'It has been a long time since we had any sweets. It might be nice to have some.'

'After all you've been through?' asked Cyril, taking his false teeth out again. 'They rot your teeth if you have too many you know.'

The Fish Fingers looked at the teeth and then at each other.

'We won't have too many. And we could have some fruit as well,' said Bel.

'And something cheesy with crackers,' said Ruby. 'And curry and chips.'

'And an enormous trifle with donuts and ice-cream in it,' said Morris.

'Right-o,' said Cyril 'It's your party!'

The elf clicked his fingers and a few seconds later the Fish Fingers sat down to the greatest sweet, fruit, cheese, cracker, curry, chip, trifle, donut, ice-cream feast they had ever seen.

STINKY PANTS

That night raindrops the size of jelly babies fell across Tumchester. The wind howled and blew tiles off the roofs and the rivers ran high with muddy water.

On a road at the very edge of town a car drove through a puddle and splashed water into a drain that was already overflowing. The drain was a hundred years old and it connected the outside world to the maze of underground tunnels and pipes that carried Tumchester's sewage to the sea. Since the iron drain cover was first lowered into place all those years ago, it had never budged.

Until now . . .

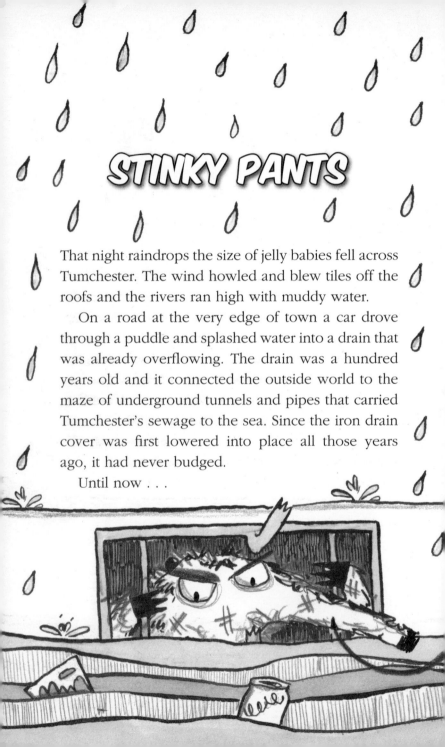

Three damp, hairy fingers crept out of the darkness below and gripped the rusting bars. They pushed hard until the ironwork moved and buckled and snapped, then they tossed it into the road. Unseen, the hairy fingers emerged from the hole and they were not alone. They were attached to two hairy hands, two hairy arms, a hairy body and a hairy head with a very long tongue. The creature stood in the road, smelling of sewage and raspberry jelly. He sniffed the air. His eyes narrowed and he smiled as he caught the slightest whiff of what he was searching for.

Pants . . .

ACKNOWLEDGEMENTS

The Fabulous Four Fish Fingers only manage to defeat the baddies in Tumchester because they work as a team and when I wrote this book, I had plenty of help too. I was surrounded by people who gave me confidence, suggested ideas, read manuscripts or sometimes just made me laugh. This is my chance to thank them. And to remind them that appearing in the acknowledgements does not guarantee a free copy.

These are the grown ups:
Kathryn Ross, Non Pratt, Liz Bankes, Mark Cameron, Michael Ward, Richard & Wendy Askam, David & Louisa Williams, Mark Nickson, Bill Haw, Bill & Amanda Finch, Mark Robinson, Jim Brassil, Sean Mohan, Sonny Hanley, Roxanne Pallett, Noel Curry, Professor Roger and Abbie Goodman, Tony Sharkey, Kevin & Sue McCarthy, Nela Willis, Dorota Mokszanska, Jon Doyle, Ian Moore, Mark Jones, Mark Barnsley, Steve Walsh, Peter A. Gordon, Phil Crabb, Lara & James Routh, Kerry Allison, Chris Twigger, Paul Gilbert, Julie Colley, Sharon Woodward, John & Margaret Merrick, Shane & Louisa Merrick, Richard & Ellen Beresford, Ashley, Chris & Gemma Beresford, Richard Hannan, Richard Marsden, Wilbert Walsh, Olwyn Moss, June Biddell, Robin & Nicki Prestwich, Brendon & Leah Guildford, Marvyn Dickinson, Ian Young, Alfie Hosker, Aunty Gladys, Roger, Anne, Andy and Roz Beresford.

These are the kids:
Hayley Beresford, Laura Beresford, Kitty Williams, Jack Williams, Seamus Mohan, Sam Brassil, Sean Brassil, Fergal Curry, Siobhan Curry, Gabriel Robinson, Henry Haw, Mitchell Sharkey, Ben Prestwich, Niamh, Grace & Erin Merrick, Josh & Izzy Beresford .

All the staff and pupils of Highfield Primary School in Leeds.